MW00874058

A LIKELY LAD

BY GILLIAN AVERY

ILLUSTRATED BY
JULIE DOWNING

SIMON & SCHUSTER BOOKS FOR YOUNG READERS
Published by Simon & Schuster
New York   London   Toronto   Sydney   Tokyo   Singapore

By the same author

Maria Escapes
Maria's Italian Spring

SIMON & SCHUSTER BOOKS FOR YOUNG READERS
1230 Avenue of the Americas, New York, New York 10020
Copyright © 1971 by Gillian Avery
Illustrations copyright © 1994 by Julie Downing
Originally published in Great Britain in 1971 by William
Collins Sons & Co. Ltd. First U.S. Edition 1994
All rights reserved including the right of reproduction
in whole or in part in any form. SIMON & SCHUSTER BOOKS
FOR YOUNG READERS is a trademark of Simon & Schuster.
Designed by David Neuhaus.
Manufactured in the United States of America

10 9 8 7 6 5 4 3 2 1

Library of Congress Cataloging-in-Publication Data
Avery, Gillian. A likely lad/by Gillian Avery: illustrated
by Julie Downing. p.   cm. Summary: Pressured by his
father to leave school for a career he doesn't want, a
nineteenth-century Manchester boy runs away and gains
a new perspective on his future. [1. Family life—Fiction.
2. England—Fiction.] I. Downing, Julie, Ill.   II. Title.
PZ7.A939Li 1994 [Fic]–dc20 92–43911 CIP
ISBN: 0–671–79867–7

CONTENTS

· I ·

WILLY'S FIRST PLUNGE

The first time that Willy Overs ran away from home was in the spring of 1895, when he was six years old. He was not, you would have thought, the sort of boy to plunge into an adventure of this sort. He was small and thin and shrinking—apt to be knocked about by larger boys—he always tried if possible to play at the girls' end of the school yard.

Besides, the world outside 19 Audley Street terrified him. Even the other side of the road seemed a wild and savage place. Rough boys lived there who jeered at him and his brother George if ever they ventured out by themselves. And through open street doors he sometimes caught sight of a mess and muddle that his mother would never have allowed.

1

But it was much more frightening beyond Audley Street. As he went to school with his mother, or to the co-operative shop in London Road, or when they all went to the Wesleyan chapel in Grosvenor Street on Sundays, he saw back streets that made him shrink up close to his mother, where wild-haired women screamed at each other from doorsteps and ragged children played without shoes, where washing hung out of windows and there were notices: "Mangling done here."

"Are those slums?" he once asked his mother fearfully, remembering the word from one of the stories they had had read to them in Sunday School. But she had told him sharply that he mustn't speak so loud.

Inside his house was light and warmth and safety. There was his father in the shop to guard them from dangers in the front. If you looked through the lace-curtained window in the door between the parlor and the shop you could see Mr. Overs' back standing behind the counter only a few inches away. And there lying on the shelf in front of the glass jars of sweets, although Willy could not see it, was The Stick, which could be used to threaten insolent boys—though boys who came into Mr. Overs' shop usually left their insolence outside in the street. And there was his mother in the kitchen at the back of the house, cooking or sewing or doing the ironing. If Willy wanted to be particularly safe he would get under the table in the kitchen, and then with the brown plush tablecloth making walls around him on three sides, he would stare at the red coals between the bars in the stove opposite, hugging his knees, and comfortably certain that here the dangerous outside world could not possibly find him.

The outside world was Manchester, but of Manchester, Willy, age six, could form no impression at all. His father told him that Ardwick, where they lived, was part of Manchester—just a little part of it. So he thought vaguely of Manchester as a world of black little houses, just like the streets he saw about him, all stuck together in long rows with chimneys puffing up lines of yellow smoke; where you hurried past the side streets for fear of what you might see there, where the buzzer called from unseen mills for the people to come to work, and called again in the evenings to send them home. This to Willy was Ardwick, and Manchester, and the whole world.

But it was into this world, nevertheless, that Willy ran that April morning, and it probably would never have happened if he and George, his four-year-old brother, had not been sitting in the parlor.

"Need we sit in the parlor?" George had said in a whining voice, hanging on to the edge of the kitchen door as his mother swooped from cupboard to table and back again, gathering up all the implements that she needed for her baking.

"You know I won't have you under my feet when I'm baking. You're very lucky to have a parlor to sit in. I've known children that were tied to the table leg when their mothers were cooking."

"I hate the parlor. It's dark. Why do we have to live on the dark side of the street? There are always shadows on our side. There aren't none on the other."

"You be thankful you do live on this side of the street, George Overs," said his mother, scandalized. "It's the respectable side. There's riff-raff on the other. You look at their doorsteps and sills. And their curtains! Proper poverty-struck they are. Now stop talking and go along with Willy."

"Can I have my soldiers, then?"

"You know quite well you can't have your soldiers in the parlor."

"The marbles, then?"

"Nor your marbles, neither. You know that as well as I do. And if you don't behave yourself and go along this minute there'll be no cake for your tea."

"Can I ask Father for some paper and pencils?" asked Willy, who, at six, had more mature tastes.

"If Father'll let you have those then that will be all right. But there's to be no mess on the floor, mind, and you're not to touch anything that's there."

Willy and George finally shut the door on the bright warm kitchen, where the April sun streamed cheerfully in. The hallway outside seemed cold and dark, so did the parlor. Willy had always disliked the parlor, except on Sundays when all four of them would be sitting around the fire. Only then did it take on a homelike, family look. At other times it was dark and stiff with plumped-up cushions perched on their points and every antimacassar spread starched and correct over the chair backs, and a look of disuse over it all.

"I'll go and ask Father," said Willy. He pulled open the door to the shop. "Father, Mother says can we have some paper and pencils?" He had to put in "Mother says" because he and George were not supposed to show themselves in the shop.

"There's some old invoices. You can use the backs of those. You'll find two pencils in the brass pot on the sideboard. You going to be in the parlor this morning?"

"Mother's baking," said Willy in a flat, disconsolate voice.

"You mind you're quiet then. You don't want me bringing in The Stick, do you?" Willy looked at his father's spiky ginger whiskers and his fierce blue eyes, and quailed.

"No, Father."

"You tell George to mind what he's about, then. We won't get Mr. Ramsbottom coming here for his cigars if the news gets around that there's boys racketing about behind the shop."

The invoices and the pencils kept them quiet for a while. Then Willy gave it up and lay on his back, staring up at the ceiling and trying to imagine what the room would look like turned upside down, making a white floor with the gaslight sticking up from the middle of it. George kept interrupting his concentration. He was doing scribbles, wavy lines like hills and valleys, and showing them to Willy and asking "Is it proper writing now, Willy?" Willy could not read very much, and could only write in crooked capitals, but he knew that writing, grown-up writing, though difficult to read, was not like that.

"No, that's not proper writing."

After a bit, George started to whine. "It *is* proper writing. Father's goes like that. I *know* it's proper writing."

"What does it say, then?"

"I don't know."

"Writing has to say something."

"Why does it?"

Willy had had enough. He wanted to be left alone with his thoughts. "I'm going outside," he said.

"Going outside" meant only one thing, a visit to the privy at the bottom of the yard. At 19 Audley Street the privy was never referred to in so many words. "Going outside" was quite enough; usually adults did not say as much as that.

From the hallway, he put his head in at the kitchen door. "I'm going outside," he said, looking wistfully around at the kitchen. It was his favorite room in the house, and after the murky gloom of the parlor it now looked particularly desirable. He liked the cupboard with its blue and white service of plates that they never used; the black shining range with its steel knobs that his mother used to burnish with sandpaper, and the high mantelpiece with the loud-ticking clock.

His mother, flushed with the heat of the range which had been stoked up for her baking, looked up from the cake pans and bowls spread on the table in front of her. "All right then, just this once, but don't you go on making excuses to go out. And mind you wipe your feet coming in, I scrubbed that floor yesterday. And whatever you do shut that door quiet and don't go making drafts or I'll have everything in the oven ruined." Then she relented. "There might be some scrapings if you and George are really good boys. You hurry up and mind what I said about the door, now."

Willy moved off. He cast a frightened look into the dank, dark scullery on the other side of the hallway, where there wasn't any gas so you had to take a candle at night when you were sent to wash. A tap was dripping now in a melancholy way into the stone sink. Then he pulled open the back door and slipped out.

It seemed so bright and sunny that he blinked. It was a fine mild morning. He and George had wanted to be outside playing, but his mother had said no, they would be in and out everlastingly through the back door making drafts and spoiling her cakes. Besides, Father had just whitewashed the yard walls, and they would be kicking dirty balls around.

Beyond the gate in the wall Willy could hear children playing in the alley that ran the length of the row of Audley Street houses. Every house had a yard behind it, and every yard opened onto the alley. It made a good playground, though Willy and George's mother wouldn't allow them there. "I'm not having you mixing with that nasty rough lot," she used to say. So their games were limited to the whitewashed enclosure of the yard.

Willy went to the yard door and put his eye to the crack by the hinges. He couldn't see anything and a whistling wind made him blink. There were feet playing hopscotch outside, somebody was kicking a tin can, somebody else was bouncing a ball. The sun and the smell of the warm, rain-washed air went to Willy's head. He drew the bolt of the door, opened it, and peered out.

The hopscotch stopped at once. "Look who's here!" yelled one of the players, a big boy of eight with a thatch of red hair. "Little Willy Overs who's too good to play with us. Ooh, don't he look sweet, don't he just, in his little woolly stockings and his nice clean boots!"

"Bet yer old man don't know you're here!" screeched another. "Bet he'd give you a leathering if he cotched you. Him and his old ginger whiskers!"

Willy looked warily behind him. Certainly he did not want his mother to hear any of this. He knew quite well that he was not allowed to unbolt the door.

"He's looking for his mammy," jeered the red-head. "Mammy's little pet in his little woolly stockings. Shall we blow his nose for him?"

"I'm going for a walk," said Willy in a trembling voice.

"He's going for a walk!" parrotted two or three voices with contemptuous disbelief.

"With his little reins to stop him falling down!" added the redhead. He was two years older than Willy and sometimes came into the shop to buy candy. He was very different then in front of Mr. Overs and within reach of The Stick.

"I'm going to the park," said Willy, and with legs shaking with fear, he marched down the cobbles. There were hoots and yells behind him, but nobody followed, and he got to the end of the alley, where it came out in Crown Street.

He just could not go back again, straight into the mob of boys. The only other way was down Audley Street and in at the shop door. But his father and The Stick were there. At the thought of The Stick his legs went faster and he ran down Crown Street.

Crown Street was very like Audley Street: the same terraces of narrow black houses with lace

curtains and a pot of aspidistra in the windows.
But the people in Crown Street were strangers to
Willy. Nobody gave him a glance, nobody asked
him what he was doing, or told him to go home.

He passed the bottom of Audley Street, running still, and reached Grosvenor Street. Grosvenor Street was a wide one, noisy with carts and
wagons and trams. You went down it to reach
chapel and the co-operative, and on the way you
passed a side street that Willy particularly
dreaded, where he had once seen a man lying in
the gutter. He turned in the opposite direction
and ran on.

He was stopped short by another road at the
end of Grosvenor Street, the one that ran north
into the city, and south, his father had told him,
into "the country." He hesitated here, aghast at
what he had done; he had hardly ever been as far
as this. But he would have to go on, because
behind him lay dangers that he could not face.
And then he remembered the park, and a glim-
mer of daring was kindled inside him.

His father had talked about the park and how
he was going to take George and him to see it as
soon as George was big enough to walk there.
What was it? he had asked. Grass, said his father,
and water and flowers—hundreds of flowers.

Who did it all belong to? To everybody, said his father, to everybody who pays his taxes, that is.

"Do you pay your taxes?" he asked his father.

"I do that," said his father fiercely.

So the park was something that belonged to his father and others like him and where there were flowers and grass like a picture book. For weeks now he had longed to see it. He even knew where it was. His father had pointed down this big road, Oxford Street it was called, and said you could reach the park by walking on out of Manchester. It was too dangerous to go home now, so why didn't he try to find the park? And here Willy discovered for the first time that if you make a move, however timid, in a certain direction, events, like a wheel, can sweep you along with them and take you up, to a point farther than you had ever dreamed.

It took Willy half an hour of jog-trotting, and he had a painful stitch in his side and aching feet before he saw what he wanted on the other side of the road. He had a strong impression of ducking very close under a horse's head, and seeing huge cartwheels inches from him, and he ran faster to get away from the voice that shouted at him and into that paradise behind the iron railings.

He had seen trees before, of course, and grass. They sometimes walked to Ardwick Green to see them behind the railings in the middle of the road. But there weren't many trees and they belonged to the people who lived in Ardwick Green. Here the place was thick with them, and there was rolling grass beneath. He was in such a fever of excitement that he couldn't stand still to look at any one thing. He just ran around and around, down the paths, around the flower beds, over the grass, until at last, breathless and panting, he scrambled onto a bench and sat with his legs dangling.

The sun felt delicious. It seemed to warm him right through to his bones without being uncomfortably hot. He blinked sleepily at the sparrows that cheeped and fluttered near his feet. He would come back here every day and sit in the sun, away from annoying people like George. But as he was turning this over in his mind, a mob of boys came sprawling down the path. He stared at them apprehensively, biting his bottom lip. They were a rough lot, ragged and dirty, and Willy's neat clothes seemed to infuriate them. They stopped and pointed at him. Willy's lip began trembling. They noticed this, too, and pressed closer. He flung himself off the seat and ran, followed by the shouting, jeering mob. Rounding a corner, he saw a bush ahead and dodged behind it. There he crouched with a hammering heart that nearly choked him. The mob went past, and he was left alone in the silence.

He looked about him. In the grass nearby was a square bed with tall flowers in it; some yellow, some white, with the most delicious scent. He squatted down and sniffed them. Nobody might know about this part of the garden. It looked so secret that he might be the only person to have discovered it. He knelt down and began picking, laying the flowers carefully beside him. The sensation of snapping through those pale green, juicy stems was utterly delightful, he could never have imagined bliss could be so great.

That was how the park keeper found him; kneeling on the path with a pile of daffodils beside him, singing tunelessly to himself, and so lost in happiness that he paid no attention to the shouting behind him. Then he found himself being shaken violently and staring up into an angry red face fringed with whiskers. He had no idea what he was supposed to have done, and when he picked out of the torrent of words the questions "What's your name?" and "What do you think you're doing?" he said that his father was Mr. Overs and he paid the taxes. Gripping him by the shoulder, the man pushed Willy ahead of him down the path. Willy tripped and stumbled, his

eyes too blind with tears to see where he was going. He was crying, not so much with fear, and certainly not with shame, but because of those beautiful flowers that had been left lying there to die by themselves.

Mr. Overs met them by the gate. Willy did not wonder how he came there. Parents always did seem to appear when you least expected them. A lot of words passed above his head. The park keeper gave him a final shake, and Willy trotted back to Ardwick, crying all the way.

· 2 ·

THE YOUNG THRUSTER

Mr. Buller was sitting in the shop when Willy and his father came back. He was sitting where he always did, on the chair by the counter, talking to Mrs. Overs who still had her apron on. Even in his state of bedraggled misery Willy noticed that, and was dimly aware of how extraordinary the occasion was, for his mother always spoke very contemptuously of women on the other side of the street who appeared in their aprons in the front of the house. You could wear your apron first thing in the morning when you were scrubbing the steps and the sills, but after that it looked, she said, proper poverty-struck.

Mrs. Overs gave a strangled shriek when she saw them. "Oh, Alfred, wherever did you find him? You've been so long I thought . . ." But she

17

never said what she thought might have happened.

"In the park, picking flowers," said Mr. Overs. And at the mention of the flowers Willy put his knuckles into his eyes and sobbed. He did this partly to drive out the sight of Mr. Buller, whom he detested. Mr. Buller had a heavy white mustache stained with yellow and eyelids that showed their red linings. He used to sit in the shop for hours on end with his bowler hat on and his hands clasped on top of his stick, listening to Mr. Overs. He had swiveled himself cumbrously around now and was staring at Willy.

"Picking the flowers, was he?" said Mr. Buller. "And running away too? They'll be sending you to the mills. That's what they do to naughty boys here. Send them to the mills."

This finally broke Willy. He let out a howl, dodged under the counter flap, and hurled himself at his mother, burying his face in her floury apron. As a small child he had always thought of mills as monsters that ate people. This was partly because of the terrifying voice of the buzzer that called the people to work there—shadowy figures with black shawls clutched over their heads that hurried with a clattering of clogs under the bedroom windows early in the morning. Now that he was older he understood that a mill was a huge building that towered up into the sky with hundreds of windows and a tall chimney that puffed out smoke. But he still shuddered at the thought of it. His parents spoke as though it was the most dreadful thing that could happen to anybody. "What can you expect, his father works in a mill!" they said about some boy Willy had seen viciously battering another in the street. And his mother said the same about people on the other side of the street who did not keep their steps and window-sills properly whitened.

After this, Willy was hustled away. He was led to the scullery where his grimy face was vigorously washed. Then his hands were smacked, and he was told that dinner wouldn't be till late because of all his carryings-on.

Damp and sniffing, he joined George in the parlor. George pressed his face against the curtains over the door into the shop. "Father's talking about you," he said.

Willy went over and joined him. Mr. Overs' back blotted out most of the view, but he could just see the brim of Mr. Buller's bowler hat.

"And what did our Willy say, with all them flowers in a heap beside him," his father was saying, "but that the park belonged to all them as paid their taxes, and his father paid his taxes, so he could pick the flowers. There's a young thruster for you! He's a likely lad. He'll go far, our Willy."

George nudged Willy. "What's a thruster, Will? If it means someone who's good at fighting, then it's a lie because I can get you down easy as easy."

Willy did not know what a thruster was, either, but it didn't sound like anything he was. But he did grasp that his father was in some curious way pleased with him. It was the first time that he heard he was a thruster and a likely lad; he was to hear much of it in the years to come, and it was to become a great responsibility.

But for the time being his destiny did not trouble him. He knew that his father talked about him to favorite customers and he was sometimes even called into the shop so that he could be shown to them. But it was not until the day that he learned to read that he became aware that his father had plans for him.

Learning to read happened quite suddenly, in chapel one Sunday. He got up for the hymn after Mr. Goodsire's sermon, and when he looked down at the hymn book which his mother had put into his hands, the words seemed to jump out of the page and hit him. They were not just black marks; they said things that he could understand. He turned to another page to see if the magic worked here too; it did. Excitedly he looked up at his mother to try to show her the miracle that had happened. He had known his letters for years, and could painfully spell his way through words if someone stood over him and made him. But left to himself he had just looked at pictures in books and dismissed the print around them as a meaningless frame. Now, without any effort of his own, the print spoke to him.

But his mother had noticed nothing of this earthshaking upheaval in his life. She was singing with deep concentration. With her eyes still on her book and not appearing to move them, she firmly turned Willy's pages back to the proper place and gave his hand an admonitory tap.

But he got his glory later. He poured out his story on the way home and his father made him read advertisements on buildings, and street names, and the words floated out of Willy without him even trying. Then, when dinner had been cleared away, they had had their afternoon walk around Ardwick Green, and were home sitting in the parlor in front of the fire, Mr. Overs pointed to the little group of books on the shelf above the sideboard.

"Willy, you're a reader now. You cast your eyes

over those books on the shelf and read me their titles."

The books had always been part of the furniture of the parlor, but they had been lifeless blocks as far as Willy was concerned, apart from the fact that neither he nor George had ever been allowed to touch them.

"There's *Self-Help* by Samuel Smiles," said Willy, peering up, "and *The Life of Cobden*, and William Cobbett's *Advice to Young Men*. And the *Wesleyan Hymn Book* and . . ."

"You can stop there. The others are your mother's books. You reach me down those first three and bring them over. Get a chair to the sideboard. Careful now."

Rather disappointed, for these looked dingy and unpromising compared with the bright colors and gilt lettering of the books which were apparently his mother's, Willy cautiously lifted down the ones he had been told to fetch and put them on the table by his father.

"There," said his father reverently, "there's all the wisdom and the knowledge you need to start you off in life. That and the Bible. Self-Help—do you know what that is, Willy?"

"Self-help, help yourself," said George from the floor where he was coloring in his Scripture outline picture. "Mother says it's rude to help yourself."

"And so it is," said Mrs. Overs. "Your father didn't mean that at all."

"Self-help," said Mr. Overs, resting the book on his lap and leaning forward in a glow of enthusiasm, "means getting on in life and not sitting down and whining and saying you can't. Some people get on in life because they're born into high places and things come tumbling into their laps. Then there's others who look on at them and say it isn't fair and squat in the dirt without lifting a finger to help themselves. And there's the others, and those are the ones Samuel Smiles wrote about, that fought every inch and raised themselves and did great deeds and became great men. And that's the examples I want Willy to have before him." Here he turned to Willy and looked at him expectantly.

Willy felt utterly unequal to the occasion. He was also embarrassed. He hung his head and fingered the other books on the table. "Cobbett and Cobden," he said. "Is that the same man, Father?"

"Is that the same man?" said his father, roused. "Willy Overs, I'm ashamed of you. What's your names? All of them!"

"William Cobbett Overs," faltered Willy.

"William Cobbett. And you still don't know who he was?"

Willy shook his head.

"There's kings who would do a lot worse than have that name. William Cobbett. He was a working boy, the son of a farm worker. But he educated himself and he wrote all manner of newspaper articles and stuff about farming and that. But what I honor him for," said Mr. Overs, clapping his hand down on the arm of his chair and leaning forward, his eyes bright with passion, "is the way he stood up to the aristocrats."

"What's aristocrats?" said George from the floor. "Mother, can whales be purple, because my black crayon broke on Jonah's hair."

"Aristocrats," said his father, "are them with a handle to their name and rolling estates and great palaces. They laid their yoke on the common man and kept him under, and if they had their way they'd still be trampling on him. It's because of the likes of men like Cobbett and Cobden who stood up to them that they aren't."

Willy felt that the glory of his hour would depart unless he took care, and struggled to find an intelligent remark that would keep the family's attention on him. "Did Cobbett and Cobden stand up to the . . . the aristocrats like we stand up at school when the teacher comes into the room?"

For a moment Mr. Overs did not comprehend. Then he slammed his fist down on the table with such force that Mrs. Overs looked at him startled, and George sat up from his crayoning and stared. As for Willy, he knew that his glory had vanished now, and he hung his head and hoped that he would not cry.

"Get to their feet for the aristocrats like a pack of schoolchildren? Men of the likes of Cobden and Cobbett kowtow to that lot?" he shouted. "Why, do you know what Cobbett called people as did that? Base toadies of a clodpole aristocracy, he called them. And as for Cobden, he *lived* in Manchester, just up the way from here. So if you don't know about him, it's high time you did. He was one of them who brought about the downfall of the aristocrats and the wicked Corn Laws!"

"Do aristocrats ever come to Ardwick, Father?" said George, impressed by his father's oratory, and abandoning Jonah and the whale. "Would you fight them if they did?"

"I'd fight them if my duty lay that way. But with my tongue, not with a sword. But they don't come to Ardwick nor to Manchester neither. The air don't suit them, don't suit them at all." Mr. Overs' grand manner was beginning to slide off him;

he was back in a good humor now, and Willy, relieved, ventured to look at him again.

"Anyway, we'd soon have them out on their noses if they did come," said Mr. Overs robustly, "so don't you worry, Georgie boy."

"I'm not worrying," said George. "Mother, my purple's broke now. There's only red and green and yellow left. What's best for the whale?"

"Will you tell us about when you were a little boy, Father?" asked Willy. Mr. Overs was mopping his forehead after all his speechifying, and this request, Willy knew, was always well received. Besides, he liked hearing about it.

"Well, what do you want to hear?" Mr. Overs leaned back comfortably in his chair, and stuck his thumbs into his waistcoat.

"About how poor you were then, and how you made your way."

And so Mr. Overs told them the story that they already knew well, but it always made Willy and George very secure and comfortable to hear it because it had a happy ending. The early part was sad, of course, but it was so long ago that it didn't really matter. Mr. Overs could not remember his father, who had died when Mr. Overs was four, leaving his mother to struggle to bring up three children (there were twin daughters younger than him) as best she could in a cellar room in Ancoats. Willy and George had never been in Ancoats, though it was only a few streets away, but they knew what a poverty-struck place it was; there were a lot of mills there too. As soon as he left school Mr. Overs had had to support the four of them, for the twin sisters were always ailing after the rheumatic fever they had had, and were never likely to be able to work. He had had jobs as a warehouse lad, an errand boy, and did washing up for one of the big hotels in the middle of the town. Sometimes one job in the daytime and another at night, always contriving to save just a bit every week, though sometimes it was no more than a penny. The sisters had died, first one, then the other, and his mother soon after, and he had been an orphan when he was fifteen.

"An orphan," said Willy, as he always did at this point. It was hard to get used to his own father being an orphan; orphans were a storybook idea.

"Yes, an orphan. I had to stand on my own feet then—not that I hadn't been doing that since I first walked. There wasn't anybody in the whole of Manchester who cared what became of Alfred Overs. But I didn't let that bother me. I just went on, working, working, working, always putting a little bit of money away, always with the idea that one day I was going to be my own master. Until, here I am, my own master and my own landlord, with a nice little business, and the best wife and the best boys in the whole of Ardwick." And here he put his arm around Willy who was standing near him, and leaned over to give Mrs. Overs a smacking kiss.

"Well, times are different now, no doubt about that. When I think of the treat it was to have herring for tea, or to find that the pie shop was selling off stale pies for a penny! And how sometimes if I felt flush I'd go up to Shude Hill market late on a Saturday evening with five-pence in my pocket and buy two pennyworth of vegetables and threepennyworth of scrag end of mutton to make a stew. And here we are with meat for our tea every day, and a full larder, and no worry about where the next meal's coming from. And just like I'm telling you now how I worked to raise myself, so you two boys will do the same for your sons. Particularly Willy, I've great hopes of Willy."

This was a new departure, and the boys both stared at him. "Willy's not going into the mills then?" said George. "Like Mr. Buller said that time he ran away."

Again Mr. Overs slammed his hand down onto the plush tablecloth. "Willy go into the mills!

That's a fate that will never overtake either of my sons while there's breath in my body!"

"I should think not, indeed!" said Mrs. Overs. "Why, I'd never be able to hold up my head again."

"No," said Mr. Overs with his eyes fixed dreamily on the ceiling, "Willy's going to start where I left off. He's got the stuff in him to do it, I can see that. He's going to climb up and up, and we're going to watch him and be proud that his name is Overs, William Cobbett Overs. So you open that *Self-Help*, Willy, and let's hear you read from it. It's not too soon to begin listening to the wisdom of Samuel Smiles."

It was the first of many such readings. Only usually Willy did not read very much of it himself because he always got attacked by a violent fit of yawning which would make his father, exasperated, snatch the book from him and read aloud himself. "A great man's words deserve better than yawns," he would say.

Sometimes Willy listened, and sometimes he let the words flow over him, part of the comfortable evening sounds in the kitchen, together with the click of his mother's needles as she knitted round after round of black stockings for him and George, the clink of cinders falling into the ash pan, and George's murmurs as he lay on the floor marshalling his toy soldiers. He supposed he would understand about getting on in life and helping himself when the time came, but he hoped the time would never come; he was very happy as he was, and he wanted nothing changed.

· 3 ·

THE NORTHERN STAR

Very little did, in fact, change until Willy was eleven. It was in that year, 1901, that the Northern Star came into his life. It was that year, too, that he first became fully aware of the great rivalry between the Overs and the Sowter families.

Mrs. Sowter—Auntie Kitty—was Mrs. Overs' sister, the only relation she had in the world, and it was the tradition that the Sowter and the Overs families should exchange visits on the first Sunday of every month. On one Sunday the Overs would catch a train which would take them to Trafford, the select Manchester suburb where the Sowters lived, and the following month the Sowters, with an air of disdainful condescension, would take the train from Trafford and walk down to Ardwick.

The house at 19 Audley Street would be burnished from top to bottom before a visit from the

31

Sowters. It always was polished up on Fridays as a matter of course, in readiness for the weekend. But the preparations that went on before those six first Sundays of the year, the other first Sundays being spent, of course, at Trafford, were especially thorough. If Mrs. Overs could have contrived it, she would have re-washed all the front doorsteps and sills and lace curtains of the whole of the street too, so that Ardwick could put up a good showing for the Sowters. It was always her grief, too, that she could not give her parlor that beautiful unused look of Auntie Kitty's. In Audley Street you had to go through the parlor to reach the shop from the rest of the house, whereas Auntie Kitty kept hers as a holy place for most days in the year.

On that particular Friday afternoon early in September, two days after school had begun, George and Willy came bursting in soon after four o'clock to find the kitchen empty, though fierce with heat from the stove.

"I'm here," called Mrs. Overs from the parlor. "I won't be long. I'm just hanging up the curtains."

They found her in her apron, hanging the lace over the door to the shop. "I'm all behind today. I just can't catch up with myself. Did you smell my baking when you came in? I'm afraid that oven may be too hot."

"It smelled all right," said George. "Cor, I'm hungry. What's for tea?"

"There's precious little, I'm warning you. What with it being first Sunday you'll have to put up with what you get."

"Oh, it's first Sunday, is it," said George crossly. "Then I wish it wasn't." He sat down on the sofa and leaned back against the cushions. Mrs. Overs whirled around with a screech.

"George Overs! What do you think you're doing leaning against my cushions that I've just put straight! You get up this minute."

"I'm hot," grumbled George. "It's like an oven outside. It isn't fair having to go back to school when it's like this. And I wish there was something to drink except water that's always warm like it is in the scullery." But he got up all the same and wandered over to the sideboard where Willy was standing reading. "What's that you've got your nose in?"

"One of Mother's books," said Willy, giving his mother a cautious glance. Normally the boys never touched the books on the shelf without permission—permission that George would never ask for anyway; he never opened a book if he could help it.

"You just make sure your hands are clean, that's

all I say." Mrs. Overs was now wrestling with the curtains over the street window, and that and the heat probably stopped her from taking the book from him as she usually would. The three books that stood at the end of the row, *The Children's Tabernacle, Ministering Children,* and *Alice Leigh's Mission,* were her Sunday School prizes from long ago, and nobody was ever normally allowed to read them.

George peered over Willy's shoulder, "What's that, Will? At the beginning?"

Willy turned back to the fly leaf. It had a brightly colored bookplate pasted on it. "Joseph Street Wesleyan Chapel," it said, and then written in careful copperplate, "Ellen Chaffey, prize for good attendance."

"Ellen Chaffey? Who's that?" said George blankly.

"Mother, of course."

"Chaffey? What a funny name. I didn't know your name was Chaffey, Mother."

"Well, it was," she said shortly. "And now you've seen it, you shut up that book and leave it where you found it."

"And was Auntie Kitty's name Chaffey, then?" George persisted.

"It was. Have you done as I told you?"

"Yes, Will has. Who was Grandpa Chaffey then? You never talk about him."

"He died long before you were born."

"And Grandma Chaffey too?"

"Yes."

"Then you was an orphan then, like Father? Who looked after you?"

"We had an aunt. Now George, I'm telling you ..."

"Is she dead too?"

The heat, the stretching up to the curtain rod, and George's persistent questioning had all combined to snap Mrs. Overs' temper. "George Overs, I've just had enough of all this! Going on and on like this with me nearly dead on my feet and first Sunday the day after tomorrow and my work not a quarter through. You go into the kitchen this instant and if I hear a squeak from you I'll get Father to fetch The Stick—I'm telling you that straight."

Even George had the sense not to talk anymore about the Chaffeys to his mother, nor about the Sowters either. He held his peace on Saturday too. Anyway, it was so hot, far too hot for much talking. For September it was scorching weather, far hotter than it had been all summer, and the sun made the pavements feel red-hot and seemed to use up all the air in the house. Dinner on Sunday was cold, or as cold as it could be made in this weather, and had been put forward half an hour, to give them plenty of time to clear away in the kitchen and lay the parlor table for tea.

"It would be nice if Uncle Harold and Auntie Kitty forgot to come for once," said George, as he looked at the table spread with preserves and potted beef and ham and hard-boiled eggs and pickles, to say nothing of the Eccles cakes and custard tarts for which Mrs. Overs was famous. Willy looked at him, shocked. He had often thought the same, but he knew that this was not the thing to say.

Mrs. Overs was outraged too. "George, that's a wicked thing to say, and you know it. On a Sunday, too, when you ought to be feeling good to everyone. Now you and your father and Willy had better be off to meet them. It would never do to be late for Uncle Harold."

It was early yet, far too early for the train, but they always had the uneasy feeling that Uncle Harold, by sheer force of will, could urge on trains to arrive hours ahead of the timetable. The street outside was like a furnace, though the house had seemed hot enough. The pavements scorched through the soles of the boys' boots. Their black woolen stockings fretted and irritated the backs of their knees. Their collars chafed their necks. The belts of their thick Norfolk jackets cut into their middles. It made them all feel irritable, and this was probably why George started on his questions. He must have known they were awkward ones.

"Father, who do you think does the best tea? Mother or Auntie Kitty?"

"Mother has the best touch in baking, she always had. No doubt about that. Those custards of hers! Even Uncle Harold would have to say that. But I suppose your Auntie Kitty can spread herself more, as you might say."

"Yes," said George, mentally comparing the two teatables. "Her trifles have real cream, not custard. And the size of ham she has—cor!"

"But I don't think your mother would like you to be talking like this," said Mr. Overs reprovingly. "Not on Sundays, anyhow."

They went on down the desert of Grosvenor Street, which was lapped in Sunday emptiness. They were dragging their steps, partly because of the heat, partly because there was so much time in hand. George returned to the attack. He never cared much what he said—a fact which often acutely embarrassed Willy, who had much more sense of the proprieties.

"Father, why does Uncle Harold and that lot

carry on as if we was dirt? Because we're not and one day I'm going to tell them so."

Mr. Overs was outraged by this. He came to a standstill and his voice echoed around Grosvenor Street. "Sowters treat us like dirt? I'd like to see them try! Overs are as good as them any day, and I'm ashamed that a son of mine don't see it."

"But I didn't say . . ." protested George, shrill with indignation. He didn't have a chance against Mr. Overs' indignation.

"They may live in Trafford and all that, and your Uncle Harold may be the kingpin of Mirk and Drabble, or so he's always telling us, and drive his own trap when he's traveling for the company. But I'm telling you that in the end he's their servant. I wouldn't want to be the servant of no one, not I. I'd rather be like what I am and call no man master, and shut up shop when I choose. And as for that Stan of theirs learning Swedish drill and chemistry and bookkeeping and shorthand at his Commercial Academy for Young Gentlemen—I reckon that young Willy here at his school is in a fair way to outstrip him already. And that's what you ought to be a doing of, George—applying yourself to your books and trying to get on and get the better of young Stan instead of talking about Sowters treating us like dirt!"

After that tirade there was silence; nobody even grumbled about the heat. In silence they waited at London Road Station, Willy thinking all the time, as George had already said, how nice it would be if the Sowters proved not to be on the train. Then they could happily go back to Audley Street alone and have a pleasant time by themselves with their mother all calm instead of on edge as she was with the Sowters, and their father reading aloud to them out of the *Sunday Companion*.

But you could not keep up this hope for long after the train had arrived, because Uncle Harold was so immediately obvious, no matter how many other passengers there were. You could see him at once, shouldering his way through the jostle, and Auntie Kitty and the cousins trailing after him like a string of barges.

Uncle Harold was huge, a monster of a man, thickset as well as tall, with a bull neck, a red face, and hands the size of hams. He looked as though he had gorged on beefsteak and stout all his life. And no doubt he had. Auntie Kitty kept a good table, and her whole life was dedicated to watching Uncle Harold with frightened anxiety, and trying to keep him in a good humor. He had a loud, roaring voice, and it was difficult to say when he roared loudest, in his good moods or his bad. In the first he laid down the law and told everybody their business, and the noise he made was so great that there was no point in anybody else speaking. In the second he picked on just one person, and that one person wished he was dead while the rest of the listeners sucked their teeth and thanked their lucky stars that *they* weren't being demolished too.

Mr. Overs was not a small man, he was lean and spare and upright, but he seemed to shrink in Willy and George's eyes when Uncle Harold was around. The sharpness went out of his ginger mustache, and the authority out of his voice. The other Sowters, though in a lesser degree, seemed to be superior beings too. Auntie Kitty's clothes rustled more and had a finer luster than her sister's, and she behaved as though Mrs. Overs was somehow to be pitied. The cousins all went to school at very select establishments: Stan, who was a little older than Willy, went to his commercial academy, and the girls, Lily and Dolly, both younger, were at a school for young ladies and learned dancing and drawing and French.

Stan, a thick, stolid boy with a huge appetite, was the only one of the Sowters who did not seem terrified by Uncle Harold. That was not to say that he ever went against his father, of course. It was just that when the Overs saw him on first Sundays he seemed able to go on eating and ignore his father's moods, which the females of the family could not do. Let Uncle Harold get excited, and their food would lie untasted on their plates. Lily and Dolly, wispy creatures with tow-colored hair and pale blue eyes, spoke as though they had a permanent cold in their heads, though Willy could not remember a word they had ever said to him. They opened their mouths if an adult addressed them, and that was all. Lily and Dolly drooped their heads lower and lower over their skirts when their father was angry, until you thought they wanted to leave them there. As for Auntie Kitty, she watched him the whole time with the nervous blink of her pink-rimmed eyes that never stopped.

But on this particular Sunday Uncle Harold was in one of his good moods. When he came striding up to the ticket collector he was actually whistling, even though it was Sunday, and he did not mutter with exasperation when Dolly found that her bootlace was untied, and stooped to tie it.

"Well, Willy. Well, George," he shouted at the boys, turning his big bulging eyes on first one and then the other. "Been good boys, eh? Is your mother keeping well?"

The boys muttered something, offered the sides of their heads to be kissed by Auntie Kitty, and looked at their cousins. Lily and Dolly immediately lowered their eyes; Stan stuck his hands in his pockets and scowled.

"Well, Harold," said Mr. Overs. "Comes around quick again, first Sunday, don't it. Seems like no time at all since we were last here waiting for this train. Now I just wondered, seeing as how you live out in the country and things are a bit quiet, I daresay, whether you wouldn't like to take a little stroll into town and see the shops."

He was, Willy could see, trying to assert the superiority of city life to life in the select suburb of Trafford, but even Willy could see what a mistake that was. Trafford was superior, there was no doubt about it. It lay on the edge of Manchester, and no sound of a buzzer or of clogs disturbed its tranquility. Its houses had gardens back and front, some of the roads had trees in them, and beyond the Sowters' house in Chester Road lay the Blind Asylum, the Royal Botanic Gardens, and then the football and cricket grounds. It struck the good humor out of Uncle Harold at once—the idea of him being pitied for anything! Him, Harold Sowter, who lorded it over every other commercial traveler on the road! The afternoon was off to a bad start. The procession wended its way over the hot pavement with no one talking except Uncle Harold, who had got Lily and Dolly in front of him and kept on telling them to get a move on or he'd be falling over them; and to pick up their feet and hold up their heads.

In this fashion they trailed along the hot street until they reached the Royal Infirmary. To reach the shops they would have to pass in front of it, cross the road at the far end and then make their way down Market Street. At the sight of the huge expanse of flagged pavement in front of the infirmary, and with the thought, no doubt, of the scorching heat of its surface, Auntie Kitty wilted.

"If you don't mind, Alfred, I don't think I'll go no further. The weather quite takes the life out of me, and seeing as it's Sunday I don't think it's quite the thing to go looking in shop windows."

"Quite right, Kitty, quite right," said Uncle Harold loudly. He did not often support his wife, but here he was getting a hit in at his brother-in-law. "Besides you can come into town to the shops on your own any day."

"There's my feet too," said Auntie Kitty faintly.

"Then you just sit down here on one of these benches for a minute or two." Uncle Harold looked ferociously at Mr. Overs to remind him that it was all his doing, and then went over to one of the seats that stood on the infirmary pavement and flapped at it with his hat. "You sit down here a bit. It's a nasty place and not what I would choose, but there it is."

Giving Uncle Harold a startled look, as though she did not usually get this sort of treatment, Auntie Kitty sat down with a gasp of relief, fastidiously lifting her skirts a little from the litter of dirty paper that surrounded the bench. It was indeed a nasty place, and not at all where you would expect a family from Trafford to be sitting on a Sunday afternoon. The benches outside the infirmary were the haunt of the undesirables of Manchester. On the bench, a little farther along, a shifty trio was eating scraps out of a greasy bag, with a bottle on the pavement in front of them. Beyond that, sprawled full-length and snoring loudly, lay a bloated heap of rags clutching a bottle in an inert hand. Willy thought that Auntie Kitty's feet must be nearly falling off if she could bear to sit among this.

His father must have felt much the same. He tried to make some sort of apology. "I'm sorry, Harold. It just came into my head that you might like to see a bit of life."

"If you call this filthy junk 'life,'" bellowed

Uncle Harold, jerking a thumb at the other occupants of the benches, "then Ardwick must be a worse place than I thought it was."

"It was the shops that I meant," said Mr. Overs, with dignity. "Living in the country as you do, you perhaps don't have the same chance as us in the city."

This enraged Uncle Harold. At the top of his voice he pointed out that Trafford was not the country, otherwise he wouldn't be living there, would he? Trafford was a select residential area, that was what it was, and let anyone tell him what the city had that Trafford hadn't. Shops? They could come in by train anytime they wanted. As for Ardwick, who in their senses would live there if they could live anywhere else?

Having settled Ardwick, he passed on to the country. What an unwholesome place the country was. How he wouldn't live there for all the gold you could offer him, nor none of his family neither. Here he glanced around at Auntie Kitty and his children with a quelling look. Women might talk about the dirt of towns, but what he said was, it gave them something to do, didn't it, cleaning it off. Kept them out of mischief. And when did a bit of soot do anybody any harm he'd like to know. It gave flavor to the air, that's what it did, and anybody who didn't believe him—he looked around aggressively with his huge, bulging, bull-like eyes—should just go and have a lungful of country air; nasty, empty, cold, damp stuff that it was, fit to stupefy anybody. No wonder that country folk were all such bumpkins.

During all this the children stood in a row behind the seats. Stan defiantly had turned his back on the adults and was scrutinizing the great black pillars of the infirmary and the life that came and went through the doors beyond them. The girls smoothed out the creases in their gloves and fingered the pleats in their dresses. Willy, trying to ease the pressure of the collar on his neck with a hot finger, stared glumly at the blue serge across Uncle Harold's shoulders and wondered how it took the strain.

In fact, he considered Uncle Harold's shoulders all the way home. Uncle Harold had worked himself into a thoroughly good humor again with his denunciations of the country. And forgetting, apparently, all his concern for Auntie Kitty's feet, he led the procession back to Ardwick at a cracking rate. Willy trotted behind him. He was by now so fascinated by his uncle's shoulders and the way the muscles moved under the cloth that he fell into a sort of dream and walked right into Uncle

Harold when the party came to a halt preparatory to marshalling itself to cross the road.

Behind him the two girls sucked in their breath with alarm. But Uncle Harold still hadn't got over the good mood that had spread over him since he had trampled on Ardwick and shown up the country for what it was.

"Well, young Willy, you in love? Walking all over the place without looking where you're going. Don't seem to have heard much from you this afternoon. What have you been up to? How old are you now? Eleven, is it? Time to be thinking what you're going to do when you leave school. What are you going to do, eh? Help your father in the shop?"

Pushing Willy in front of him, Uncle Harold marched across the road. There was a horse tram coming in the other direction, but Uncle Harold paid no heed to that. He shook his arm at it in a threatening way and called on the others to stir themselves. Willy shrank under his grasp, but his uncle did not slacken his grip.

"Well then, what's it to be, eh?" he repeated, giving Willy a shake.

"I want to live in the country," said Willy faintly. He had not the least idea why he said it. He just let out the first thing that came into his head and hoped that it would mean his uncle would leave him alone.

To everyone else and to Uncle Harold himself, however, it sounded as though Willy was deliberately setting himself against his uncle. There was a horrified intake of breath, followed by silence.

Then Mr. Overs spoke. "I don't know what our Willy's thinking of, talking daft like that. He's going to go into the Northern Star, the insurance business, you know." He pointed up at the huge building, looking as though it was carved out of coal. Adorned with complicated windows and pillars and carvings, all pitchy black, it made that part of London Road very dark, and Willy always felt as though he were walking into cold shadows when he passed under it.

Of course everybody knew what the Northern Star was, without Mr. Overs telling them. But no one, least of all Willy himself, had ever connected Willy Overs with it.

"And what'll he do there?" said Uncle Harold at last. Even he seemed to have been winded by this piece of information.

"Oh, he'll start as a clerk, I daresay, and work himself up to better things." Mr. Overs gave a twirl to his mustache ends.

"Flying a bit high, ain't you?" said Uncle Harold.

"Oh, our Willy's up to it," Mr. Overs said airily. "Doing well at school, he is. I'll be having a word soon about him with Mr. Ramsbottom. That's the chief clerk, you know. Comes to the shop regular for his cigars. Oh, we'll see our Willy manager of that concern yet. He's got drive, that lad. Do you remember the time he ran away and picked the flowers in Whitworth Park and said they belonged to them as paid their taxes? There's a lad for you!"

The party was now moving down Grosvenor Street on its way to Audley Street and tea. Willy was stumbling along at the back, bemusedly contemplating this entirely new scheme for his life which his father had just so coolly presented. Stan waited for him.

"You be manager of that lot!" he said. "You couldn't manage a duck pond. Is Uncle Alf saying it for a laugh or what?"

George, already irritated almost to frenzy by the strain of a first Sunday, the discomfort of an over-starched collar, and the heat of the pavement, spoke up. "Father's not one that says things for a laugh!"

Stan sniggered. "Ay, that he's not. Wouldn't dare, neither, not to our dad."

George, goaded out of his usual easygoing temper, reached for Stan's ear, and twisted it for all his worth. It could not have hurt Stan all that much;

he was three years older than George and built on his father's massive scale. But he chose to let out a savage yell, punch George full in the face, knock him back against a house wall, and there continue pummeling him. The two fathers, roused by George's crying and the tinny screams of Lily and Dolly, turned to find George sprawling limply against somebody else's front door, with blood pouring down his face, and Stan struggling against the restraining hold of his sisters, while Willy was staring at it all "like one of those country bumpkins that your Uncle Harold was on about," as his father said later.

· 4 ·

THE NICHES IN THE TOWN HALL

Willy remained in his bemused state during
the whole of that "first Sunday" tea.
The commotion that everybody else was making
about George and Stan's fight passed right over
him; he was concerned with his own affairs. He
had never in his life thought about what might
happen to him when he left school. Indeed, he
had always had a vague idea that growing up,
going into long trousers, earning his living, was a
thing that might happen to other people, but certainly not to him. And now here was his father
speaking as though all these things were not only
inevitable, but about to happen tomorrow.

He emerged from his dream when his father
gave him a dig. "Didn't you hear what your Uncle
Harold was saying?"

Willy shook his head dumbly. They were all sitting around the tea table, laid out for the occasion in the parlor on Mrs. Overs' best white teacloth, the one edged with tatting that she had done herself. Tea was over, it seemed, and everybody was sitting silently around the remains of a spread of which not much had been eaten.

"Well, listen, and don't act so dumb. Uncle Harold asked whether you and George would like to go with him and Stan to watch the football at Old Trafford one Saturday."

Willy, appalled, stared at Uncle Harold's bulging eyes. It was not just that he did not like football. He was paralyzed at the thought of having, for the first time, to face Uncle Harold without his parents as a line of defense.

"Haven't you got a tongue in your head?" demanded his father.

"Thank you very much, Uncle Harold," Willy faltered. He stole a glance at George to see how he was taking it. George, his face now cleaned up, but with smudges of blood still on his collar to remind the Sowter family of the injuries that one of them had inflicted, was staring at Uncle Harold with the same consternation. And Uncle Harold had his thumbs stuck into his waistcoat pockets and a smug expression of duty well done.

The Sowters took their leave soon after that.

Auntie Kitty and Mrs. Overs offered their cheeks to each other.

"I'm sorry about . . . you know," said Auntie Kitty almost tearfully. "It won't stop you coming to Trafford next first Sunday, I hope?"

"Well, we'll have to see what Alfred says." Mrs. Overs looked in the direction of the shop, where Mr. Overs was holding up the counter to let the guests out into the street. "But I shouldn't hardly think so. It was the heat, don't you think? Makes children act peculiar."

But this was not the line she took when once the Sowters were safely on their way down Audley Street and the shop door bolted behind them. She did not attempt to clear the tea, but sank down in her chair and, to Willy and George's consternation, put her face in her hands so that you could almost have thought she was crying.

"The shame of it! On a Sunday too! I'll never be able to hold up my head again! All those people on the other side of the street standing at the door in their shirt-sleeves and no ties so Harold could see them and all! Oh, it makes my flesh creep when I think of it! And me always trying to show Kitty and Harold that we can keep ourselves respectable in Audley Street just as much as people do in Trafford!"

"Well, seeing as it was Harold's boy as did the

damage, I don't see why you need take on so," said Mr. Overs.

"But all that rough lot coming out to look, and the others on our side standing behind their curtains and looking, I'll be bound. What will Harold and Kitty be thinking? Bad as anything in Gorton or Ancoats, it was."

"What they ought to be thinking is that their boy ought to have a touch of the strap. Going for his little cousin like that."

"Uncle Harold gave me a threepenny, Father," said George, unclenching a sweaty fist to show it. "He's never given me nothing before."

"And he's taking you to the football. First time Harold's ever put himself out for anybody, I reckon. He was fair rattled by Stan's goings-on, I could tell that. Hardly had a word to say at teatime. Not for him, I mean. Heard the sound of my own voice for once."

"But the *neighbors*," moaned Mrs. Overs, approaching from a new angle. "All that screeching and yelling. There wasn't a soul in Audley Street, or Crown or Paradise for that matter, as could have missed it. And that Mrs. Jericho two doors down that keeps herself so proud, there'll be no holding her now. I shouldn't be surprised if you didn't find trade dropping off and us having to leave Ardwick."

"Don't you worry, my girl," said Mr. Overs, thumping her on the back. "Trade's pretty snug. And what do you say to our Willy being in the Northern Star! That's what I said to Harold. I've always had it in the back of my mind that Willy was going to move up in life, not work in a shop or anything like that. Then when we were standing by the Northern Star it came over me quite suddenlike, that was where our Willy was going. Stands to reason when you think about it. Us knowing Mr. Ramsbottom and all. There's plenty of room there for a lad to get on and climb right to the top of the tree. You wait, Harold Sowter, in a few years you'll be wishing our Willy was your Stan!"

And, alight with his hopes and his plans, he pulled down *Self-Help* from the shelf and sat astride a chair to expound it while Mrs. Overs dolefully cleared away the tea things. It was going to take more than the thought of Willy's bright future to sponge out from her mind the shame of that afternoon.

"Listen to this, Willy. 'Some of God's greatest apostles have come from "the ranks." The poorest have sometimes taken the highest places; nor have difficulties apparently the most insuperable proved obstacles in their way.' Did you hear that, Willy? There's gold for you. You take that up and store it away. You go on forging ahead and then perhaps someone will make an example of *your* name. And you be thankful you weren't born a blue-blooded nobleman. There wouldn't be anything to work for then—lapped in luxury, fed with a golden spoon. You show them what an Overs can do! Honest labor is the best teacher; the school of toil is the noblest of schools. That's what Smiles says, that's what I say!"

And he brought the front feet of his chair down to the floor with a crash. "I tell you what, Willy. We'll go to the town hall this very next Saturday, just you and me. Mother won't mind staying in the shop for an hour or two just this once, I daresay. I've got something to show you there, Willy, something that will act as the star to guide you to high places!"

But what it was he refused to say. It was George, though, who pressed to know. Willy felt uneasy about the whole affair and hoped that perhaps by Saturday the matter might be driven from his father's mind. There was no chance of that, however, with George's persistent questioning. George was at the age when he always did say the things you most hoped he would not. When Saturday came, Mr. Overs had made elaborate plans for their mother to take over the shop. She didn't like the idea at all, and eventually it was arranged that she should sit in the parlor and only go in when she heard the sound of the bell on the shop door, and that she should explain to their regular customers that she was only doing it this once to oblige.

It was a great occasion when Mr. Overs walked down Audley Street that Saturday morning with Willy. It was the first Saturday he had been out of that shop, he told Willy, since he bought it twelve years ago. He was in tremendous spirits and swung his walking stick and talked to Willy about the splendors of Manchester and the privilege of being born a Manchester boy. "What Manchester thinks today, Willy, London thinks tomorrow! You remember that when you're a great man and the smart folk from London boast about where they live. I'm going to take you to see the house of a man who chose to live in Manchester because he thought there was no better place for him while he fought the battle of the common man against the aristocracy. You know who that is, Willy?"

"Would it be Cobden, Father?" said Willy, hesitatingly. As a small boy he had always mixed up Cobbett and Cobden, to his father's intense exasperation, and still was uneasy about them.

"It is Cobden. Richard Cobden, the enemy of the privileged, the friend of those who toil for their bread. What a man!"

To reach Quay Street, where Cobden had lived,

they had to go up Oxford Street into the city. This was a rare event for Willy who usually only went into town with his mother and George twice a year, once to see the lighted shops at Christmas, and once to see the Whit processions. He would have liked to dawdle and look in shop windows, but his father marched relentlessly on. By the time they reached Quay Street, Mr. Overs was, to Willy's eye, in an alarming state of emotion. They had just passed the site of Peterloo. He was recounting again, with a throbbing voice, as Willy had heard him do scores of times before, the story of the Peterloo martyrs, who had met to ask for a fair deal for the working man and had been mown down by government troops.

"They asked for fair government, Willy, that was all they asked for, those starving men, maddened by the sight of their starving wives and children. Fair government, not much to ask for, you'd say. But my lords in London thought otherwise. What did they do? Sent a troop of cavalry to ride down those starving men, mowed them down like corn before the reaper, trampled on them, slashed at them with swords. It was a terrible thing, Willy, a truly terrible thing!"

But Willy was only conscious of the curious looks that passersby were giving them as his father

shouted and gesticulated. "Did Cobden live somewhere near here, Father?" he ventured, trying to
divert him.

"He did, Willy. With Peterloo a stone's throw
from him. Here you are, Richard Cobden's house.
He fought to get bread for the common man, to
repeal those Corn Laws which taxed the loaves of
the starving so that the aristocrats might put diamonds in their shoe buckles. If I met a man who
had done a twentieth as much for the human race,
Willy, I'd drop down to him on my knees in the dirt
and kiss his hand!"

And Mr. Overs, carried away by the fire of his
own oratory, cleared his throat and wiped the back
of his hand over his eyes. Willy, glancing at him
furtively, wished uneasily that he would have done
with Cobden and with Peterloo. Then, feeling
guilty, he fixed his eyes on the house outside which
they were standing. But there was so little to
remark about it, except that there was one large
black footprint on the white-stoned surface of one
of the steps. Willy started wondering how it had
got on that step and no other and what his mother
would have said about a footprint like that on her
front step.

Striding out to try to keep up with his father as
they marched to the town hall, Willy felt that he

had failed. He ought to have been able to produce one remark to show his father that he was a rising light, who was going to emulate Cobden, Cobbett, and Smiles, and put Stan Sowter in his place, but he could think of nothing at all.

The town hall was huge. It reared upward with complicated rooftops, and spread outward with thousands of windows, filling the whole of one side of Albert Square. Mr. Overs' mind, however, was not on the town hall yet. He was pointing out the statue of Cobden.

"There you are, Willy, the Apostle of Free Trade; Manchester's tribute to one of her great men. Mark it well, Willy, and remember the date that you first saw it."

But Willy, staring obediently at the begrimed figure on its pedestal, could only think how uncomfortable it must be to have pigeon droppings all over you like that. He followed his father into the town hall. His father was taking off his hat as if it was chapel, so Willy took off his too, and stood gazing about him in awe. Immense marble floors with pictures in them spread in front of him; the people who were scurrying over it seemed like midgets in comparison and their voices just a murmur in the vastness of the place. There was a staircase grander than anything he could have imagined, two sets of stairs coming down facing each other, and where they met, becoming one staircase. He felt his father was expecting some sort of response from him.

"It's like a palace, Father," he said weakly.

"It's a palace of palaces, Willy. There's not many as could boast a place like this, I can tell you. Do you know how many cubic feet of stone went into it? 480,000. And 16,500,000 bricks. Just think of it, Willy! And how many masons would you say worked on it? Think, Willy."

"A million?" hazarded Willy feverishly.

"Seven hundred," said his father severely. "A hundred more than ever worked on the Houses of Parliament in London. What do you think of that now?"

But Willy could only think that the numbers didn't sound anywhere near as big as they ought to be. "It's very big," he said feebly after a long pause. "I like the floor and the stairs. Thank you for bringing me, Father."

"But you haven't seen what I brought you here for. What I told you about last Sunday. You come over here."

Beckoning Willy, he led him to the wall on one side of the door through which they had just come. It was lined with niches which held the busts of rather fleshy men with whiskers.

"Is one of them Cobden, Father?" ventured

Willy, faintly. "Or Cobbett or Smiles?" he said wildly, sensing that his first guess was hopelessly wrong.

"None of them," said his father with irritation. "No, Willy, what I brought you to see were *those*!" Holding Willy's shoulder he pointed with a trembling finger to a group of empty niches beyond. But here Willy's powers of improvisation, such as they were, completely left him. He looked blankly at the niches, and then blankly up at his father's face.

"There's one there reserved for *you*, Willy boy. Nobody knows yet which one it is. But one day, I'll come in, an old, old man, and I'll point to one of those niches that Manchester keeps for her most famous men, for those who have served her with glory, and I'll say that's my Willy! And they'll say, Sir William Overs—you'll be knighted by then, Willy. You know him? And I'll say, know him? Why, he's my son!"

· 5 ·

TRAFFORD ON A SATURDAY

On his way home Mr. Overs enlarged on his plans for Willy's future. He frequently blew his nose, much moved by his words. Willy was to raise himself into a position of great importance in the Northern Star, and from there he was to step into public service, Councillor he would be, Alderman, Lord Mayor, and finish up by having streets and hospitals and schools named after him, and his bust in the town hall. He went on about this at dinner time when they got back.

"Can't you do all these things if you've got a shop, Father?" asked George toward the end of the meal, shoveling up his treacle pudding.

"Course you can," said Mr. Overs stoutly. "Manchester's glory is her trade, and there's plenty who's risen from humble beginnings here."

64

"Then why don't you have a try, Father?" George demanded, lovingly licking every vestige of treacle off his spoon and contemplating it between licks.

"Because it's too late for me. I did my bit in putting enough behind me to buy my shop—and I can tell you there weren't many boys of my sort who would have managed to earn an honest living, let alone put enough by to have his own business. But you boys are different, I've taken care to give you a good start, and I only hope I'll live to see you make use of it."

Willy had always been given to daydreams, and now he had an entirely new theme for them—Sir William Overs, in velvet robes and gold chain, advancing with stately dignity down the splendid staircase in the town hall, toward expectant crowds waiting on the marble floor below. It buoyed him up for several weeks, and even carried him through the ordeal of the October first Sunday at Trafford. No need for him to feel ill at ease now as he usually did in Cromwell Villas. He could sit serenely gazing at his plate, thinking that the time would soon be coming when the whole Sowter family would be enviously discussing his banquets at the town hall.

But the daydreams failed before the prospect of

that football match in Uncle Harold's company. It was not going to be forgotten, either, as Willy had so passionately hoped; that October Sunday the fathers made the final arrangements for the following Saturday.

One afternoon on the way back from school, he asked George whether he wanted to go.

"No!" said George violently, giving the wall a kick.

"Why not?" persisted Willy. "You're keen enough on football, Stan and you."

George stared at him with incredulity. "Because of Uncle Harold, that's why. You're afraid, same as me, aren't you?"

"Ah," said Willy. That was what he wanted to find out. The boys had never discussed Uncle Harold before. Schoolmasters you could discuss, and other boys, and customers who came into the shop. But discussing the family was like discussing the Bible—something you never dreamed of doing. He also felt uneasily that somebody who was going to climb to the top of the Northern Star and rule Manchester from its heights ought not to be afraid of a mere uncle. First Sundays were all right, he could lurk in the shadow of his parents, but going to Trafford without them made him feel like a snail without its shell.

His father seemed to realize something of this. "You just hold up your head and don't let no Sowters get the better of you," he said next Saturday, when he was giving Willy the money for the train fares and a labyrinth of instructions about how to get on the train, how to get off, how to find his uncle, and how to come home. "And remember, not so long now you'll be having the laugh on Stan." He stood bareheaded in the street waving goodbye to them. They looked back for a last time when they got to the corner by Crown Street and he was still there. Willy felt almost like running back then, to the safety and security of home.

But the journey by themselves was easier than their father had made it seem. The train rattled above the roofs of the city. Willy peered around the burly youth next to him and stared out the window, fascinated by the glimpses into backyards and bedroom windows. If only he could just go on and on with no Uncle Harold and no football to spoil everything.

Uncle Harold and Stan met them at Cricket Ground Station, and they pushed their way through the jostling throngs unloading themselves there. Once up in the stands at the football grounds Uncle Harold was settled into a good humor for the afternoon. The stands were packed already. It was difficult to see where three boys could be squeezed in. But Uncle Harold was not daunted. He stood in the gangway, regardless of the people coming up the stairs who pushed and jostled impatiently behind him. He cast his eyes slowly around the stands, made his choice, and moved purposefully forward.

"Here, you," he said grimly to a collection of cloth-capped men with red and white mufflers. "That's my place, you hop it."

And they went. While Willy and George watched, stupefied, those four men slunk off. They didn't raise a murmur between them, and the people around them didn't either. Uncle Harold sat himself down with a satisfied snort, and his satisfaction lasted the whole of the match.

His satisfaction with himself, that is; he had plenty to say about the football. "Call that a kick? I've seen a jellyfish could do it better!" "And the trouble with this lot is they ought to be playing puss in the corner with their sisters." He went on like this loudly and ferociously all through the game. Nobody seemed to mind; several people turned to agree with him. Willy, wedged between George and an excited youth with a noise maker, was far enough from his uncle to feel safe. He could almost enjoy himself, watching the players scampering about the pitch below and listening to other people getting the rough end of Uncle Harold's tongue.

Tea afterward at Cromwell Villas in the Chester Road was much more of an ordeal. The Sowters lived in such a superior house. It was only attached on one side, it had a bit of garden in the front, and a door that opened into a hall, and not, of course, into a shop, as in Audley Street. There was a front parlor that nobody went into during the week and it had a piano in it. There was a front kitchen where they took their meals, a back kitchen for the cooking, and a scullery and wash-house that stuck out at the back.

Though the Sowters did not behave at table very differently from his own family, Willy always had the uneasy feeling that they might, and he watched his cousins warily in case he wasn't holding his knife the right way. But it was the cousins who got into trouble, not him. Uncle Harold had been carving a round of cold beef with great dexterity and speed and sending plates filled with it down the table.

"Please, Pa, may I have only a very little?" bleated Lily.

Uncle Harold stopped carving and glared at her ferociously. "I don't like girls that pick at their food and moan. What's the trouble now?"

"Please Pa, I'm not hungry."

"You weren't hungry yesterday, nor the day before that, nor the day before that neither. What's wrong with you, I'd like to know?"

"There's nothing wrong, Pa. It's just that I don't want much meat," faltered Lily. Willy could hear tears in her voice and a lump came into his own throat out of sympathy.

Uncle Harold hit the table a thundering whack with his red, ham-sized fist. Cups rattled in their saucers, knives danced about the plates. "If there's nothing wrong and you aren't ill then why can't you eat your victuals proper, curse it. There's nothing riles me more than picking and moaning and complaining. You'll eat your beef or I'll know the reason why."

But at this Lily buried her face in her pinafore and wept, and Dolly out of sympathy put hers up to her eyes and gulped and sniffed too. A moment or so later they were hustled out of the room, and could be heard dismally climbing the stairs, hiccuping with sobs. Willy was very glad when he and George had to leave soon afterward to catch the train home.

Stan was sent to conduct them to the station. "And you just mind you hurry back," Auntie Kitty called after him. "There's your piano. You haven't done it yet."

"Will you get it from your dad if you don't get back in time?" George asked with a certain amount of awe. This was another thing that marked off the Sowters. They had a piano, and all three cousins had to learn. They played their pieces for the Overs on first Sundays. The pieces didn't seem to change much from one month to another as far as Willy could tell; it always seemed to be the same old thing that was being thumped out, and you always had to hold your breath in the same places while they wrestled to collect up their fingers for the louder thumps.

"Not from Pa, not over that," said Stan contemptuously. "It's Ma as minds about piano. And she's only going to mind when I'm at school. When I'm free of school I'll be free of that too. I'd like to kick the old piano under a train."

"I'd like a piano," said Willy suddenly.

"Whatever would you do with it?" asked George, astounded.

"I dunno. I'd pick out tunes maybe. And I'd like to see what it sounded like when you played notes together." Willy had never considered a piano before but now that he began thinking about it the possibilities seemed limitless.

"Oh, Will," said George, with a certain amount of scorn, "he's always on about some fancy or other. Stan, those men in the stands. Did your dad know them?"

"What men?"

"Them as he gave the shove to."

"Course he didn't."

"Why did they get up then?"

"Because he's Pa and he's a thruster. He always sits in that place, and if anybody gets there first, then they have to go, that's all."

"Cor," said George, slowly mulling this over in his mind.

Stan became expansive. "You can't get nowhere unless you're a thruster. People just push you out of the way. I'm going to be like Pa, in the traveling line like him, and drive my own trap. But you've got to have push to do it."

"Our Willy's going to get on," said George aggressively. "Father says so."

"*Him*," said Stan contemptuously. "I tell you you've got to have push to get on. Look at Pa, that's how he sells so big. Last week he went to Underhill's at Eccles and told them they ought to take this new canned soup he was carrying. Told the manager loud, he did."

Willy could imagine Uncle Harold standing

there on the shop floor, his huge blue serge legs straddled, his gold watch chain strained across his waistcoat, thumbs in his pockets, his eyes glazed and staring, "telling it loud" to a shrinking manager.

"And do you know what they said at Underhill's when he told them they ought to take a case of soup? 'Not a case, Mr. Sowter.' Here Stan put on a mincing, high-pitched voice. 'We don't reckon in dozens at Underhill's. Send us a cartload.' People will always do what Pa wants because he speaks loud. Catch your old Willy speaking loud. He'll never get nowhere."

"He's going to be Lord Mayor. Father says so. Father knows what's what," said George clenching his fists.

"*Father!*" Stan made a derisive gesture. "Who's he? Keeps an old candy shop in Ardwick. Look at him and Pa. He's frightened of Pa, anybody can see that."

Fury surged in both his cousins. This was something you didn't do, talk about other people's fathers. It was also a shock, like a douse of cold water, to hear your father discussed as though he was an ordinary man. The unexpectedness of the attack winded Willy. He had no words to hurl back. He would like to have said how he hated

Uncle Harold and his popping eyes, his loud voice and his straddled legs, and how he'd like to throw him, not the piano, under a train. But this of course was impossible.

George however was a more ruthless fighter, and once he lost his temper there was no holding him. He was also two years younger which made a difference in what he dared say. "Look at your mum. She's frightened of your dad. I'm glad I haven't got a mum what's frightened of my dad. She looks as though she's fair scared of being leathered sometimes."

George had hit the nail on the head all right. Stan became wild with rage and aimed a blow at him. "You mind what you're a saying, young George. That may be the way things go on in Ardwick and in your dirty old street, but it's different in Trafford, I can tell you. No wonder Auntie Maggie won't have nowt to do with your mum. Fancy living in a place where you have to go through a shop to get into your house! Why, you'll even have to be carried out through the shop in a coffin when it's time to get buried!"

He aimed another swipe at George, who ducked, and then strode off the way he had come. George, stirred more than Willy had ever seen, screamed after him. "Going back to play your piano like your mammy says? Rotten old Trafford, rotten old Sowters. Your dad's nothing but a big bully." George was beside himself with fury and hopped from one foot to another. He paused, because he was hoarse, and there was no more abuse left in him. Willy seized him by the arm.

"Stop it. Come on or we'll miss that train."

"Blubbering sisters. Stinking Trafford," screeched George at the now distant back of his cousin. He was not going to stop while there was wind left in him to shout. As a final gesture he did what their mother had brought them up to believe was associated only with the lowest and roughest boys from the worst streets: he put his fingers to his nose and thrust out his tongue. Then, sobbing with rage, he yielded to Willy's pulling, and went with him.

· 6 ·

Auntie Maggie

Willy and George did not say a word all the way home. In the train they looked uneasily in different directions, reluctant to meet each other's eyes. It was terrible, the things that had been said between them and Stan down there near the station; Willy felt dirty all over.

Mr. and Mrs. Overs were still sitting over tea in the kitchen when the boys came in. Mr. Overs had his watch on the table in front of his plate.

"There you are, then. If you hadn't come in five minutes I'd have been down to the station to find out why. Well, how was it? Do you want some more tea? Though I reckon your Aunt Kitty's given you a right good one already, hasn't she?"

The boys stood in the doorway hesitating. The lights had not been lit yet. The fire beside the range gave off a red glow between its bars, and through the window the black roofs of houses were silhouetted against a reddened sky. It looked warm and peaceful.

"Come in and shut the door," said Mrs. Overs. "And sit down if you want some more tea."

The boys came to the table but sat sideways, to show they were not there to eat. There was an uneasy silence.

"Well," said Mr. Overs impatiently, "aren't you going to tell us nowt?"

"You haven't been fighting with your cousin again?" put in Mrs. Overs, scrutinizing their faces.

"No, we haven't been fighting, have we, Will?" George gave a hasty, wary look at his brother. "Stan took us to the station but he had to practice the piano after we'd gone," he rattled on. "He says he wants to throw the piano under a train. Lily and Dolly have to practice too. They cried at tea because Uncle Harold gave them too much meat."

"I don't want to hear about pianos and girls crying." Mr. Overs banged his cup down into the saucer. "I want to know about the football game and how you two boys got on by yourselves on the train."

"They've been up to something, you mark my words," said their mother with female insight.

"That's why they're acting so odd."

"Will wants a piano," said George hastily. "He told Stan he did. To pick out tunes on, he said." He paused, and then burst out: "Father, who's Auntie Maggie? Stan said there was an Auntie Maggie who wouldn't have nowt to do with Mother. He was telling lies, wasn't he? Because we've got no aunt except Auntie Kitty. Rotten old Stan." His face was flushed and his lip was trembling, and he glared around the table.

It shattered the tranquility in the kitchen. Mrs. Overs got up weeping, there was no mistake about it, and left the kitchen. Willy sat scrunching the corner of the tablecloth into a tight ball. Why hadn't he made a pact with George not to talk about this to anybody. On the way home he had felt that the quarrel was too horrible to discuss with George—and now look where his squeamishness had got them! Their father tugged at his mustache points in silence.

"We won't say no more about this," he said at last. "You see how it upsets your mother. Now I'll go and put the shop to rights and you boys clear away and wash up for your mother. Then we'll have a nice game of ludo."

George had an easy temperament and it did not take long for him to put all this behind him.

"Will, that Auntie Maggie Stan talked about is dead, isn't she?" he said when they climbed into the bed that they shared. He gave Willy a kick on the shins. "She is, isn't she? That's why Mother cried, because she's dead."

"I suppose so. Why can't you get your toenails cut if you must kick?"

"I can bite some of them off with my teeth," said George with satisfaction. "Bet you can't. Rotten old Stan telling lies like that. Rotten old liar I'll call him next time I see him." And he turned himself noisily around once or twice, like a dog settling himself on a mat, and was almost instantly asleep.

But Willy could not sleep for a long time. His brain pounded, his body fidgeted. He had never seen his mother cry before. All that evening she had been acting peculiar, with red-rimmed eyes, not saying anything, and Father had been uneasy, watching her. He felt as though there were something at work cracking their family apart.

By next morning the whole episode seemed to have dropped clean out of George's mind. But Willy could not forget it. Furtively he watched his father and mother. There was something wrong. The bustle with which his mother usually attacked the housework was not there. His father's spirits were affected too; he was subdued, quite unlike his normal self. He still could lecture the regular visitors to the shop, but at meals and in the evenings he was worried and uneasy. Willy fretted himself over it, picking at his food, lying awake at night. All the comfort of home had gone, destroyed by one remark of Stan's.

At last, after a night during which he did not seem to close his eyes, Willy made up his mind. He would have to ask his father what Stan had meant, and why it had upset his mother. But even when he had worked up enough nerve to ask, it was surprisingly difficult to find the right moment. It had to be after school but before tea, when his father was still in the shop and his mother was in the kitchen. But every time he left the warm haven of the kitchen, where his mother was ironing on the table and George was fiddling with the flatirons on the range, he found his father with a customer.

It didn't take long for George to notice his coming and going. "What's wrong with you, Will?" he said idly, holding up an iron to test its heat, and then trying it out on the curtain. "You've been in and out of that door hundreds of times."

His mother, who was shaking water on an overdry tablecloth, paused with her hand in the bowl. "Is it something you want in the parlor? You've got a cold too. Don't you go hanging about in drafts or you'll get one of your bad ones. George, you put down that iron this instant. There'll be scorch marks on the curtains and then there'll be trouble."

"There's just something I want in the shop," Willy muttered, and shut the kitchen door before anything could be said. In the half-light in the parlor he pressed his face to the glass pane. He could see his father's arms flailing the air as he addressed Mr. Buller. Mr. Buller propped himself on the counter and puffed great clouds of smoke from a hooked pipe with a silver band.

"As long as we have these lords and their friends in high places the country'll come to no good. Stands to reason. For one, they don't know what work is—never smelled it in their lives, never got within a mile of smelling it. For another, they don't know what chaps like you and me is thinking. They don't know and they don't care," Mr. Overs said and banged the counter so heavily that the canister of peppermints danced.

"Willy, you come in out of the cold," called his mother faintly from the kitchen.

"Just coming," he called, and pushed the door open into the shop. His father swung around in irritation. He didn't like being interrupted when he was in his speech-making vein.

"Why, Willy, what do you want here?"

Mr. Buller pulled himself up and took his pipe out of his mouth. "Reckon I'd better be going, Mr. Overs. There's business to be attended to." Slowly, ponderously, he made his way to the door, pulled it open, held up his face to the weather, knocked out his pipe, stowed it away in his pouch, and then with heavy deliberation, shut the door behind him.

Willy watched with feverish impatience. "Father," he gabbled urgently when Mr. Buller had moved off at last, "Who is Auntie Maggie? Why did Stan talk about her? What was wrong between her and Mother?" He gulped in air, and stood gasping at his boldness. His eyes even wandered to the shelf where The Stick lay, and he wondered whether his father might not seize it and threaten him.

But his father had grasped his mustache ends and was twisting them. "That's no question for you to be asking."

"But have we got another aunt?" persisted Willy wildly. "You always said they were all dead."

"Aunt Maggie Chaffey," said his father hesitatingly, "your mother's aunt that is—"

But he was to get no further. The parlor door was pulled open, and there stood his mother. There was a guilty silence. Willy felt his face turning beet red. All his resolution left him; he pushed past his mother and pounded upstairs. There he flung himself on the bed and crammed his hands over his ears so that he could hear nothing that was being said in the shop below.

He was still lying like that when George came up much later.

"You'll get it," he said as Willy struggled to sit up and blinked at him in a dazed way. "Lying here with your boots on. Anyway, you're to come down to tea now."

Willy fumbled to try to straighten the bed-spread. "Are they all right?" he asked hesitatingly. "I mean, Mother?"

George was astounded. It was like asking whether the sun had risen that morning. "Of course she's all right. Why wouldn't she be?"

Willy was only partly reassured. George was not much of one for noticing. He came down slowly. There was the sound of water splashing into the stone sink in the scullery and his father singing. That in itself was odd; his father was not given to singing, except in chapel. He peered out of the scullery door, drying his hands vigorously on a striped towel.

"We've got a piece of news for you, your mother and me."

Willy stopped. He was frightened now of the

question he had asked. "What is it?" he said apprehensively.

"Aha, that would be telling," said his father in a jollying-on voice that sounded more like Mr. Goodsire at the chapel than like himself. "Let's ask Mother." He threw open the kitchen door. "Willy and George want to know what our piece of news is. Are you going to tell them, Ellen?"

Mrs. Overs was busying herself at the range with slices of ham that sizzled and spluttered in the pan. "You better tell them, Alfred. It's your affair."

"Well," said Mr. Overs, "what do you boys say if we have a piano in the parlor?"

There was a long silence. "A piano?" said Willy at last, faintly.

"Yes, a piano." Mr. Overs' manner was now becoming rather testy and more like itself. "It was only the other day as George here was saying you wanted one, Willy, and now you're acting as though I said we'd keep a zebra in the parlor."

George found his voice at last. "A piano, like Uncle Harold and Auntie Kitty's? Why there isn't anyone that's got one in Audley Street, except that Mrs. Jericho."

It was the right thing to say. Mr. Overs stroked his mustache complacently. "Well, business is good, and your mother's been wanting one for a

long time. And I don't see why we shouldn't hold
our heads as high as Mrs. Jericho. Now, let's have
some ham, Ellen. The noble lords of England can
eat their finicking caviar and peaches off gold
plates, but ham is the stuff for an honest man."

Upstairs in bed George said, "Will they make us
practice like they do Stan and that lot? What does
practice mean anyhow? Stan seems to hate it."

"I don't know."

"I don't want no piano."

"It's for Mother."

"Why?"

"I don't know."

"You're acting like Father said we're going to
keep a zebra in the parlor!" George gave Willy a
thumping kick with toenails that still had not been
cut, laughed raucously, and fell asleep.

But Willy could not sleep. His thoughts were
boiling inside him. They boiled most of the night
and stopped him from sleeping. Then around
three o'clock (he heard it striking faintly from St.
Luke's in Rutland Street) he knew what he was
going to do. He was going over to Stan's house and
he was going to ask him straight out. Tomorrow
was Saturday and he could go. But if only he could
set out now instead of spending seven or eight
hours turning over in his mind what he was going

to say to Stan and what Stan's answer might be.

He left the house as soon as breakfast was over, clutching the shilling he had pried out of his money box. He didn't tell anybody he was going out, he didn't feel he had wits enough to compose a convincing excuse. He got on the train at London Road, and off at Old Trafford station. It was not far from there to Chester Road, but it was strange to be going that way on a morning, and by himself.

Cromwell Villas looked very trim and unwelcoming, as though it wanted nothing to do with people who came from Ardwick. He wondered if Stan and all of them were standing there behind the windows shrouded in lace curtains, watching him pick his way over the red and black tiles of the path. It was Lily who opened the door for him. She was holding a duster in her hand and she gawped at him with her mouth held wider open than usual, as though he were a tiger escaped from a menagerie. Then she went lumbering down the hall, leaving him standing foolishly on the doorstep. There was a smell of baking in the air. Newspaper was laid over the carpet in the hall and up the stairs. It was a new view of the house; he had never seen its weekday appearance before.

The kitchen door opened and Auntie Kitty

appeared, rubbing floury hands on her apron. Behind her hovered Lily, calmer now that her mother had taken over.

"Well, my word, Willy, I never thought to see you here on my baking morning. What was it you were wanting? There's nothing wrong at home, I hope?"

"I came for Stan," said Willy. Then followed a pause that felt like five minutes while he groped in every corner of his mind for a reason. "I wondered whether he could come for a walk. It's a nice day."

It was not a nice day. It was a typical Manchester autumn morning, with a damp feel to the air, a yellow sky, and a dingy darkness that had never lifted since dawn. But Auntie Kitty did not contradict him. She seemed much more put out by a completely new situation with which she had never been called to deal before. "Stan go for a walk?" she said. "Well, I don't know I'm sure."

At this point the parlor door opened and Stan's head appeared. This *was* a situation that Auntie Kitty understood. "You go back in this moment, Stanley Sowter. You've done just three minutes of your practicing, and you haven't played a note for the last five. I heard you."

"That's fifty-seven to go, then," said Stan. "What does Willy want? Fancy him coming here all by himself without his daddy to show him the way."

Auntie Kitty ignored this sally of wit. "He's come to take you for a walk, he says." She spoke doubtfully.

Stan took advantage of her hesitation. "All right, then, I'll go," he said briskly.

"Not till you've done your practicing, you don't. If Willy wants to sit with you in the parlor while you do it then I suppose he can. But not a word out of either of you, mind, and I'll be leaving the kitchen door open so's I can hear. Fifty-seven more minutes you've got, and you look sharp about it. Lily and Dolly have to practice before your Pa comes in and wants his dinner."

Stan and Willy shut themselves into the parlor. It was very cold. Willy perched himself on the edge of a settee with a buttoned back and a slippery seat so hard that it felt as if no one had ever sat there. Stan revolved himself on the piano stool once or twice and stared derisively at Willy. Then he gave a shuddering sigh and turned toward the piano.

"Tell us when a minute's gone," he said hopelessly and started pounding away.

It was a very long fifty-seven minutes for Willy. He hardly dared shift his position in case Auntie

Kitty stormed in and berated them both. Not that she was a one for storming usually, but she took her parlor and the practicing seriously. He stared out at the yellow sky, though it was difficult to see much even of that with the ferns on the table and the green plush curtains drawn half across the windows.

Stan hammered away gloomily. He did scales and then pieces which he played through over and over again, making exactly the same mistakes in exactly the same places. In between he groaned and muttered. At last it all came to an end. For about the twentieth time he peered over his shoulder at the huge black clock on the mantelpiece, and this time he gave a whoop. "Two-and-a-half minutes to go. You count them for us, Willy."

In a low voice, conscious that Auntie Kitty had the kitchen door open, Willy counted aloud.

"Faster than that, that's not seconds, that's hours," muttered Stan, hammering away.

"A hundred and forty-nine, a hundred and fifty," wound up Willy.

It sounded like Stan lifted his hands off the keys in the middle of a note, slammed down the piano lid, and put his head out the door. "Finished. Your turn, Lil," he yelled down the hallway. Then he pulled a muffler off the hat stand by the front door and wound it around his neck. "C'mon then," he said over his shoulder.

The front door slammed behind them and they tramped over the red and black tiles. Stan walked fast until the house was out of sight. "You never can be sure with Ma," he remarked. "Might change her mind and say we was to stay in, or run to the shops for her. Well, what do you want then?"

He stared at Willy with curiosity out of brown eyes that bulged like his father's. Willy quailed.

"It was about what you said last Saturday," he ventured at last.

"What did I say last Saturday then?" Stan was bristling. "You ask young George what *he* said. If Pa had heard half of what young George said he'd be walloping the living daylights out of him. Oh, yes he would."

"That wasn't what I meant," said Willy desperately.

"Then what did you mean, I'd like to know?"

"It was what you said about somebody's aunt."

Stan had suddenly become very wary. "What about whose aunt?"

"Well, who is she? The one you talked about?"

"Cor, nearly thirteen years old and don't know what an aunt is. Where do you go to school? Stinking old Ardwick, I suppose. That's what happens to people that lives in Ardwick, never heard of aunts. Your aunt, young William, happens to be your mother's sister, or your father's maybe. Do you know what a father and a mother is?"

"You know what I mean. The one you talked about."

"I know what you meant, I'm not so slow as you seem to think. There's no need to judge others by yourself. What I want to know is what you want to know. You ask about aunts, I tell you what they are. Perhaps you can't think what a mother or a father is. Perhaps you think your mother hatched out of an egg?"

Willy was crimson with frustration. "Course I don't."

Stan gave a whoop of laughter. "I think you do though. Willy Overs thinks his mother hatched out of an egg," he shouted to the street at large. "Willy Overs thinks . . ."

Willy, goaded into fury, gave him a sock across his front with his arm which made Stan double up, winded. "I'm going back to ask Auntie Kitty. If it's Mother's sister, then it's Auntie Kitty's too."

When Willy said this he had no clear idea of what he was meaning to do. It was rage that made him speak as he did. But it worked. Stan didn't even hit back; he grabbed Willy by the arm and held him fast.

"Not so fast, you don't. If you talk about what we've been saying, there'll be trouble. And you know it, otherwise why'd you come sneaking over to Trafford and not ask at home." He gripped Willy's shoulder until it hurt and pushed his face very near.

"I'm not going to say anything to anybody. I just asked you."

"All right then." Stan looked over his shoulder. "You come along with me."

They had been walking up Chester Road toward town again. Stan pulled Willy on faster. He dodged down the next turn, then the turn after that, and finally scrambled down a muddy embankment. A stretch of canal lay at the bottom, black as ink, looking as though it was deep enough to swallow up the mean houses that stood above. There were flecks of foam on it, and on the banks here and there people had left their rubbish: a bathtub without a bottom, rusty pails, and bits of bedsprings.

"Here," commanded Stan, "under that bridge."

About a hundred yards down there was a bridge over the canal and Stan plunged toward it. "There," he said. "And if I think you're going to do any sneaking, I'll throw you in."

The thunder of a train overhead made Willy jump and made further talk impossible. It was a horrible place to be. Water dripped down the walls. It always seemed to have dripped there. There was a bright green stain down the blackened brick. People had scrawled things on the walls and carved their initials. Willy seemed to feel their eyes staring through him as though they were there themselves. He shuffled around, trying to keep clear of the scummy puddles on the damp path.

"Well, out with it, what do you want to know?" said Stan aggressively when the rumble and vibration above them was over.

"You said something about an Auntie Maggie who won't have nowt to do with Mother. Who is she, then?"

"She's her aunt, of course. Her father's sister, if that makes it easier for you."

"What, the one she lived with until she was married?"

"That's right."

"She's alive then?"

"That's what I'm saying."

"They've always acted as if she's dead."

"So she is, dead to all you," said Stan with relish.

"Why won't they talk about her then?"

"Because they're ashamed, and because she

won't have nowt to do with any of you," said Stan complacently.

Willy stared at him. His legs felt shaky, he wanted to stop Stan saying any more, but it was too late now. He knew he would go on asking questions until he had heard all Stan had to say. "What do you mean she won't have nowt to do with us?" he persisted.

"Your mum married lower class, that's what I mean," said Stan. "Auntie Maggie didn't like it, see."

"How do you mean, lower class?" Willy faltered. He felt very near to tears now. He hated his questions, he hated the answers, but something drove him on.

"Well, who is your dad?" asked Stan contemptuously. "Born in a cellar, worked in a warehouse, went in for washing bottles, and keeps a sweetshop in Ardwick. Auntie Maggie lives in High Street down Rusholme way. She didn't want anybody from her family going to live up Ardwick way to sell sweets. Ardwick or Rusholme, she said, you can choose, but you needn't never expect to see me again. And your mum didn't."

Stan looked at Willy triumphantly, to see how he took it. Willy shivered. He felt very cold suddenly, and plunged his hands deep into his pockets and hunched up his shoulders. "When did she say all this?" he asked dully.

"When your mum got married, of course. When did you think?"

"Is she still alive then?"

"She is."

"Do you see her then?"

"Sometimes," said Stan guardedly.

"Then why's it all so secret? Why couldn't you tell me up there in the road?"

Willy, quite without meaning to, had scored another hit. Stan grabbed him by the shoulder again and shook him. "Don't you ever dare talk about it. Pa would fair kill me if he knew I'd said what I did."

"All right, I'm not going to talk about it. But why . . ."

"Cross your heart and hope you'll die?" said Stan, tightening his grip on Willy's shoulder and pushing him to the greasy brink of the canal.

"Cross my heart and hope I'll die," gabbled Willy. "But why did . . .?"

Stan gave Willy a final shove which sent him reeling along the path. "You know you'll die and go to hell now if you blab," he shouted, and took to his heels. It took Willy a moment or two to recover his balance, and then he went pelting after his cousin, skidding over the puddles, calling breath-lessly. But Stan had the lead. He was up the bank and away when Willy reached the bottom.

"Where does she live?" called out Willy with what breath he had left. "Stan," he screeched as loudly and as high as he could, "where does she live?"

Stan paused and looked back. "Laurel Villas," he shouted. "Now you stop hollering and hop it." And he was gone.

· 7 ·

DOWN IN RUSHOLME

He hated Stan's horrible secret. It seemed all of a piece with the dripping, slimy walls where it had been thrust in front of him. It was like that filthy, reeking canal water down there by the bridge. But whereas he had averted his eyes from the water for fear of what he might see in it, he could not leave Stan's secret alone, however much he wanted to. He sat in the train that was carrying him back to London Road, turning it all over in his mind with loathing. The gray slate roofs of the houses below, damp and glistening in the fine rain that was now falling, whirled past him. He felt like a thief, clutching these bits about his mother's life; he'd be frightened now to look her and his father in the face. And how was he going to explain where he had been all morning?

He got in just as his mother was serving dinner. But nobody was concerned about him. They were talking about the piano that his mother had that very morning gone to choose at the co-op in Downing Street. With a flushed face and a manner that was excited for her, Mrs. Overs spooned out the mashed turnips and stew, and told Mr. Overs how she had rejected the model with the candle holders. "Two pound ten extra just for those trumpery bits. I told the man what I thought of that. Ours has got pleated silk in front, and a really nice grain to the wood. I'm looking forward to working up the polish on it, I really am."

And then the conversation turned on the best place to put the piano, and how all the parlor furniture would have to be moved around. Willy's absence had either been unnoticed, or was forgotten.

The piano arrived the following week. Willy and George got back from school to find a van outside the house, a quantity of straw on the pavement, and all the boys of the neighborhood circling around. Some of the people on the opposite side of the street were standing at their doors watching.

"Here's Willy Overs. Won't his nose be higher than ever, won't it just?" shrieked an onlooker as he approached.

There was hardly room for the two boys in the shop. Two sweating men in baize aprons, their faces purple with effort, were maneuvering the piano past the counter which was raised like a drawbridge, and trying to edge it through the parlor door. Papers had been laid all over the floor to absorb their muddy tramplings, and Mrs. Overs was standing by giving anxious instructions about the walls and the paint.

"What a day for them to choose to come," she said later as she arranged the top of the piano with a white embroidered runner, and experimented with the placing of photographs on top, "with first Sunday the day after tomorrow and *our* turn too. There won't be much for your tea today, I'm telling you straight, there's all that floor to clean and the parlor to set to rights." But they all knew that she was contented as she said it.

"First Sunday again? Comes around before you've time to think. Well, there'll be a piano here for you to show to Harold and Kitty," said Mr. Overs, contemplating it with pride. "The Overs don't do so badly, eh?"

They sat in the parlor that night, an unprecedented occurrence on a Friday night. Recklessly Mrs. Overs had lit a fire there, regardless of the fact that the grate would have to be cleaned out next morning, her baking morning, and the whole room tidied anew for the Sowters. She played them the *Bluebells of Scotland* and the *Ash Grove* with slow stiff fingers, and Willy made up his mind from that moment that he was going to learn to play too. He didn't care how many hours of practice it took him. He sat there in a haze of pleasure at the prospects ahead of him, Stan's disclosures momentarily driven from his mind.

They came back in force on Sunday. He had to face Stan that afternoon, and he felt that the guilt and the shame of the secret would be written all over him. They all would be able to read it—his parents, his aunt, and his uncle. But as things turned out, Stan kept well away from him, avoided his eyes, and said nothing. It was Auntie Kitty who brought up his visit to Trafford, and even she didn't broach the subject until fairly late on in the proceedings, when she was being helped to a slice of custard cake. Something about it reminded her of Willy, perhaps it was that she had been baking custards herself last week when he arrived. Wiping her fingers genteelly on the embroidered napkin, she looked surprised all of a sudden.

"My word, it quite took me back, it did, seeing young Willy in Trafford on my baking morning."

"Willy?" exclaimed his father and mother together. They stared at him in disbelief, and Willy lowered his eyes and wound his legs around his chair.

Auntie Kitty began eating her custard cake in delicate forkfuls. "He came to see Stan, he said. Him and Stan went for a walk after Stan had finished his practicing. Not that it's a thing that Stan usually goes in for, walking. But there, Willy don't have anywhere much to walk in Ardwick so it's only to be expected that he'd like Trafford better. Still, it did give me a turn, seeing him there."

There was a silence. Willy sunk his head lower, and wondered wildly what was going to be said now. Then his father spoke up. "Oh, he's a great one for walking, is Willy," he said breezily, and launched into the familiar story of Willy's expedition to pick daffodils when he was six.

The horror of the situation, and the relief of it passing over so easily, quite winded Willy, and he noticed very little of what passed during the rest of the visit. The piano was duly admired, though Auntie Kitty pointed out the absence of candlesticks and thought they were going to find it difficult to see the music with the parlor being so dark. "But there, it probably doesn't matter that much, since neither of your lads plays." Then the cousins

sat crammed together on the settee, limply looking through the pages of bound volumes of the
Sunday Companion, which was always produced on
these occasions. Stan was in a subdued mood.
Once or twice Willy caught his eye, looking at him
in a covert way as though he were reminding him
that they both shared the same guilty secret, but
he said nothing. He didn't even play his usual trick
of tweaking his sisters' tow-colored ringlets to see
if he could make them screech out.

It all came to an end at last. Mr. Overs and Willy
walked down to London Road with the Sowters,
and left them in the shadow of the Northern Star.
His father looked up at it.

"Not long now before our Willy's there," he
remarked. "Another year at school and then he's
thirteen and he'll be starting."

"Wouldn't suit our Stan," said Uncle Harold.
"To-ing and fro-ing at the beck and call of every
Tom, Dick, and Harry. Stan's like his Pa, won't call
no man his master. Isn't that so, Stan?"

"I'm not going into no office, no," said Stan,
staring up contemptuously at the Star building
through the murk of the November evening. "I'm
going on the road like Pa. Offices are for them as
can't say boo to a goose."

"Don't you fret, Willy my boy," said Mr. Overs as

Willy and he trudged back again down Grosvenor Street. "You'll be at the top of that place while Stan is holding his hat at the back of shops waiting for orders. Get to the top of that and the world's your oyster. Mother'll be that proud of you." He hesitated, and looked warily at Willy. "You know what you were asking?"

"Yes," said Willy. He clenched his hands until the nails bit into his palms.

"Was that what you went traipsing over to Trafford to ask Stan?"

"Yes," said Willy, shifting his fingers so that the nails would dig deeper.

"Did Stan tell you then?"

"Yes."

"What did he say?"

"He said that Mother had an Auntie Maggie who wouldn't see us." Willy gulped for air, and despairingly hoped that his father would call on him to say no more. But the shame of what had been said about his father, set his cheeks on fire, and he felt that anybody could read it in him.

"Ah," Mr. Overs let out his breath in a long sigh. He tramped on without saying any more for a while. Then he spoke again. "It's hit your mother hard, that. Not that she ever speaks about it. But I know she feels it, especially when she sees your Auntie Kitty. That's why I got her that piano.

They need to hold their heads high, women. Though I'm telling you—in strict confidence, mind, just you and me, Willy—that your mother's Auntie Maggie is a wicked old woman if ever there was one, and we do well to be rid of her. It's a thing I've never said before and I'll never say again."

No more was said until they were within sight of the shop, then Mr. Overs put his hand on Willy's shoulder. "It's a snug little business, but I want you to look beyond that, Willy. I want to see you at the top of a concern like the Northern Star. That way we can make up to your mother all the business we've been talking about."

But Stan's words stuck, and increasingly they came between Willy and his daydreams about Sir William Overs. Sometimes he wondered about his mother's Auntie Maggie, why she was a wicked old woman, whether his mother looked like her, whether she felt it was shameful to be married to his father. A lot of the time he wanted to stamp on the Sowters, all of them, with their superior airs and their house in Trafford. He'd show them what an Overs could do. But then he would uneasily remember Stan's prescription for success, that you had to talk loud and be a thruster. If you had to be like Uncle Harold to get on in life, then he knew he couldn't do it.

But he did like school. He had never admitted

as much to himself before, nor did he dream of saying so to George, whose conversation on the way to and from school was along the lines of "daft old Sloppy" (Mr. Hislop was his form master), "I'd like to punch his nose, I would. I'd like to show him what I think of him and his daft old spelling lists and long division sums."

Willy, two forms higher, could see what George meant. He had gone through the grind of those sum cards, those weary lists of words like "aluminium" and "victuals," the lists of capes and rivers and mountains to be learned by heart. But now in Mr. Church's form, it was different. Instead of learning spelling they had parsing, and he enjoyed that, sitting in the quiet classroom under the hissing gas jets, carving up sentences.

They were doing geometry now, and that pleased him too. In fact the neatness and reasonableness of the Euclid propositions excited him so much that he tried to tell George about it. But George was so appalled that he had to give up. "Do you mean to say that that's what I'm going to have to do in Standard Five—all that about those letters and triangles and that? What's the use of it anyway? It'll finish me, if old Sloppy's long division don't first."

It was impossible to talk to George about lessons, to tell him how marvelous Mr. Church's English lessons were, when he allowed boys to stand up and talk about the books they were reading in class, instead of keeping to the deadening reading aloud, turn for turn. But one evening he did try to tell his father about it. He went into the shop just after closing time and fidgeted about as his father put up the shutters until he turned and asked Willy what he wanted.

"Father, I like school." It seemed a feeble way of putting it, but he could not muster any other words.

"More than I did. Them and their book-learning. Time-wasting tricks, I call them. A lad must learn to read and cast up accounts, but after that he can teach himself all he needs."

Willy hesitated; he felt almost defeated already. "I suppose I couldn't stay on at school? After thirteen I mean? I could go to a Higher Grade school, or Mr. Church did say I could try for a scholarship to one of the grammar schools and I might easily get one, he said."

Mr. Overs wheeled around, incredulous. "Stay on at school? Where's the sense of that? Why, you'd be losing precious years that you'll never get back, the best years of your life, maybe. You're going to make your mark, Willy," he said coaxingly. "How can you make your mark while you're bending over your books?"

"But there's so much I want to do," faltered Willy miserably. "There's geometry and algebra, I like those, and French too. And Mr. Church did say that if I went to a grammar school I could learn Latin."

"Latin, geometry, algebra," said Mr. Overs, speaking each word with burning contempt. "Those are fine things to be talking about. The school of life, that's what you want, Willy. Latin, geometry, algebra—they're for good-for-nothing aristocrats who can't do nowt else. But you, you're different. You can be working your way up the ladder while they're still mincing around their playing fields. You'll be half way up it while they haven't thought to leave off their scholars' gowns. Remember those empty spaces in the town hall, Willy, just waiting for your statue. Schoolboys don't get statues, but men of affairs do. And that's what you're going to be, Will, a man of affairs."

His eyes were shining now, he was flinging his arms around in his best style, launched on the flood of his oratory. Willy could no more have argued with him than he could have argued with the waves of the sea.

"Look at your brother, now," Mr. Overs was saying. "He plays around at soldiers and all that, but he doesn't think he's going to *be* a soldier. He's got more sense. A game's one thing, life's another. George knows the difference. He's not going loafing around with a pimple of a pillbox on the side of his head and saluting them as aren't any better than him—only born in a mansion instead of in Ardwick. And you aren't going creeping around with a satchel under your arm, yes-sir-ing and no-sir-ing. You've got brains, Willy, and drive. The world's your oyster, you set to and crack it open." He clapped a hand on Willy's shoulder, temporarily winded. "You see I'm right, don't you, lad?"

But Willy could say nothing, he just hung his head dejectedly.

"And there's your cousin Stan," continued his father, speaking now in a wheedling voice. "You don't want him to get a start on you, do you now? Make it into a race, him and you, who's to get to the top of the ladder first. Though it's my bet that Stan will still be selling soup and tea while you're in ermine in the town hall!"

Much moved, Mr. Overs blew his nose loudly. Willy slunk off. The thought of a life spent continually taking upward steps on ladders appalled him now. It was one thing being Sir William Overs in a gold chain, but another to be battling for it against

Stan. He didn't want to do any battling, and he knew that if it came to a race, Stan would win every time.

He tried to drive these grating thoughts away by burying himself in reading. Mr. Church had suggested that he should use the free library in Rusholme Road and borrow books, and he used to spend all Saturday mornings there, dipping into scores of volumes, and trying to come to some decision that did not involve carrying off a whole shelfful.

But the Saturday after he had spoken to his father about school he arrived at the library to find that it was closed. "Closed for stock-taking" said a notice on the door. For him there would be no access to books until the following Saturday. All the pleasure of the weekend had gone; he could not think how he was going to fill it, let alone get through the morning. He stared hopelessly at the message on the door, and then all around him. It was a dark November morning. The sky was yellow-gray; it pressed down heavily on the roofs of the houses, each with its chimney stack pouring a column of smoke into air that smelled of soot. There was no use going home; his mother was baking and would not want him around, and George would be playing a furtive game of football with the boys in the back entry. Drearily he trudged away, not thinking where he was going, just letting his feet take him where they would.

His feet took him down Rusholme Road into the big road that led north into the city and south to Wilmslow—Oxford Street, the same road that he had walked down so boldly all those years ago on his expedition to Whitworth Park. He paused, and then turned south.

He was not in a noticing mood, his mind felt stuffed with cotton. He just trudged along shifting his library books from one arm to the other and staring at the damp pavements. But something did make him look up at this particular turn, and there he saw the name: High Street. He stared at the name and licked his lips. Then he turned and strode up the road.

He was noticing his surroundings now. It was very different from Ardwick, more like Trafford. There were far fewer houses, less of a huddle. Some of them were quite big, and all had iron railings in front.

Ahead of him a baker's boy, whistling shrilly, had left his cart by the curb and was pushing open a gate. He stopped whistling, stuck out his tongue, and made a hideous face at Willy. "Had your sixpennyworth of looking?" he called. "Why don't you get my photo took while you're about it? Or if you're after something real fancy you could have one of this old crow here." He disappeared through the gate, and a tangle of privet hedge that had not been sheared for years hid him. Willy came up to the gate and peered through.

The house looked as neglected as the hedge, but it was not that that caught his eye, it was the sight of the name, Laurel Villas, painted in faded letters high up on the house front. A shiver went through him, starting at his scalp and going down to his knees, and he stared on.

Behind the tangle of privet there were raised voices; the baker's boy seemed to be having an argument with someone who was shouting at him from a window. Then came a clatter of feet and the boy reappeared, flushed and angry. "Cor, she's enough to turn the milk sour, that one. Why don't you pick on someone else for a change?" he yelled at the window. "There's another one here for you." He slammed the iron gate behind him, and then, not satisfied with its clatter, kicked it open so that it crashed against the stone border to the path and bounced back again with a crash that made it reel on its hinges. At this there was a frenzied knocking on the glass of an upstairs window.

"Knock away, you old skeleton, till the giddy old

glass falls out," said the baker's boy in high good humor now, and darted back to his cart.

The knocking on the window still went on. Willy peered through the gate and looked up. And then his eyes met the eyes of the person responsible. She looked like a witch in a white nightcap, her face pressed close to that upstairs window, mouthing things that he could not hear, and beating on the pane with her fist.

"Beautiful sight, ain't she?" yelled the baker's boy, now safely in between the shafts of his little cart. "Oh, yes you are, my pretty!" And he waved his hand derisively at the window and trundled off.

The front door opened. Willy saw it moving and dodged behind the hedge. Steps shuffled down toward the gate, and a blowsy head poked itself at Willy. "Who are you, she wants to know?"

Willy would not have given the person time to ask this if he had not, in his alarm, dropped two of his library books. Stooping to pick them up he peered at the gate. An old woman stood there, with wisps of gray hair that escaped from under a flat black bonnet. Above, the knocking on the window became louder.

"You'd better come if you don't want that window broke in."

Only the ingrained habit of obedience to his elders made Willy go back, for he was terrified. He edged up to the iron gate whose paint was dimmed by age and grime to a dull, dirty red. The old woman screwed her head around and nodded up at the window. At this the knocking died away to a thin rapping and then stopped.

"Why couldn't you have come before?" said the old woman testily. "You heard all that hullabaloo. Well, who are you?"

Willy stared at her with alarm. "I don't belong here," he mumbled. "I was just picking up some books I dropped."

"It's boys she can't stomach. Keeps jugs of water to throw at them, she does. It's not having the jug to throw at the baker's boy that put her in such a taking now. I forgot to fill it after the last lot. You be off then, and don't you go hanging around outside here unless you wants a drenching."

She nodded violently at the upstairs window again, and shuffled away. But at that moment there came such a frenzy of knocking that it seemed the glass would come crashing down on her head.

"Gimme strength!" muttered the old woman. Then she raised her voice. "He's going he says, and he says he won't come here no more and he's very sorry for all he's put you through and will you please forgive him, he says," she screeched.

From behind the window came a thin voice. "Bring him up this very minute."

The old woman seemed very put out. "Now look what you've gone and done. We've never had this before. You must have been at it good and proper. Well, her jug's empty, that's all I can say, so you'll come away dry."

"But I've got to go home," said Willy in a panic.

"And I've got to take you up to her else that window will be falling out and she'll be throwing all the furniture and what have you through it. Now don't you go keeping me waiting. I've had enough to try me already, and I'm fair breaking, that I am."

Up the path went the old woman, and behind her trailed Willy. The steps to the house were crumbling and unscrubbed, and a waft of cold, damp air hit him as he stood in the doorway. Clucking her tongue with impatience, the old woman pulled him in and banged the door shut. "He's here, he's coming up now," she screamed.

Willy wanted to throw himself at the door and get out before it was too late, but somehow he seemed numbed and unable to do anything but follow. Then there came a throaty snarling from a few yards away, and he jumped back in terror. Two shadows lurked in the darkness of the passage beyond the stairs.

"Them dratted dogs loose again. You'll have to wait now till I've got them back. Here you, be off, back to that scullery." There was the sound of a yelp, of doors banging. Willy waited and shivered. The house smelled of mold and damp; wallpaper hung peeling all around the hall, and the oil cloth on the floor and the stairs was worn into holes.

"They'd as soon eat you as look at you," grumbled the old woman as she came back. "Why she don't keep a pair of raging tigers in that scullery of hers and be done with it, I don't know. She says she wants 'em tough to keep away thieves, but one day they'll eat her up and me. Then where'll we be, I'd like to know."

She toiled slowly up the stairs. Willy, trembling, with icy, sweating hands, followed. From a distant part of the house he could hear bodies hurling themselves against a door, and then mournful, blood-chilling howls.

"There they are, at it again. It only wants her to start again and then we'll have a proper menagerie."

As if prompted by this, thunderous hammering started above their heads. "There she goes. I knew she wouldn't hold her hush for long. We're coming, we're coming," she bawled. "Can't do more than that, can we?"

"Then why can't you hurry? You could have climbed those stairs six times over by now," called a harsh, querulous voice from behind a door on the upstairs landing.

"Hurry! A fine lot of hurrying I could do on *my* legs after you've wore them out for me all these years!" shrieked the old woman. Then holding on to the banisters, she turned to Willy. "Go on, you go by yourself. She's up there in the top front. That door straight ahead of you."

Willy clutched the banister rail with both hands. He felt as though he would fall down onto his shaking knees if he let go. "Who is she? What does she want?"

"Who is she? Miss Chaffey of course. I'd have thought anybody would know that. What she wants I don't know. You'll have to see for yourself. But the water jug's empty, I can tell you that, and she hasn't got the legs to fetch more. So you'll get out dry, if nothing else."

· 8 ·

Ellen Chaffey's Son

Miss Chaffey sat in a room that was so crammed with furniture that it seemed impossible to get near her—had Willy wished to do so. But he had no such wish. He peered at her through the barely opened door in terror and dismay, trying to muster the courage to turn and flee.

But Miss Chaffey, whom he could only see as a crouching figure outlined against the light that came from the window behind her, was not giving him the chance. "You come here! You're a Chaffey, I saw you out there. I'd recognize those spindle shanks anywhere."

Willy stared and did not move. She was sitting in a bed, it seemed, a brass bed that had been pushed up against the window, and on a bamboo table beside her was a huge jug. He particularly noticed this; it seemed a queer thing to want near your bed. Miss Chaffey, who had a stick in her hand, gave a menacing thump on the floor. "You come in and shut that door. Come over here, I say."

Reluctantly Willy edged forward through the slender passage that had been left between the massive bits of furniture—sideboards, a wardrobe, tables, chairs with the upholstery spilling out of them, all of them covered with a dank bloom and smelling of dust and decay. There was a fire in the grate, and a chipped white enamel bucket of coals beside it, but there was no heat in it, and it did little to drive away the damp which seemed to soak the room.

"Come closer!" screeched Miss Chaffey. "And for pity's sake move faster on those spindle shanks of yours. There, you can sit at the bottom of the bed."

Chaffey confronted Chaffey. He saw a scraggy face with yellowed, wrinkled skin under a grimy, frilled nightcap tied under her chin. With one hand she was holding a torn, purple shawl together at the chin.

"Yes, you're a Chaffey all right. Nobody but a Chaffey has hair that sticks up at the back of his head like that. Well, who are you?"

Hardly knowing what he said, Willy told her,

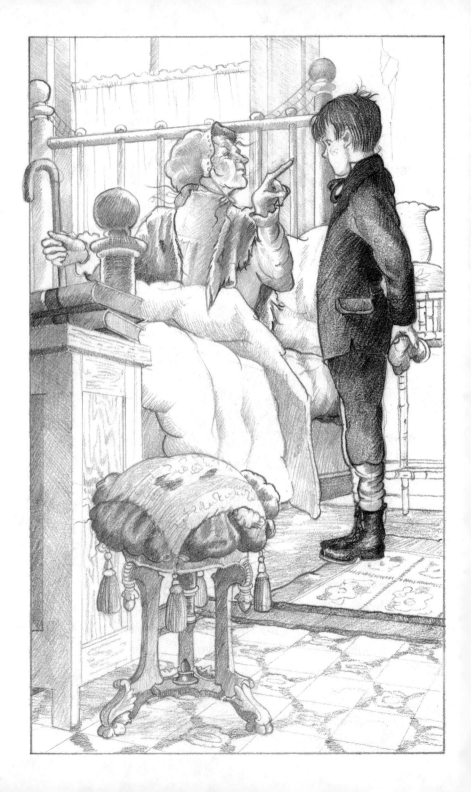

"I'm Willy Overs. I'm Ellen Chaffey's son."

"Ellen Chaffey's son!" she said in a lower voice. She seemed startled and fell back against the tumbled pillows piled behind her. Then she sat up and pointed a lean, accusing finger. "I suppose you know that's why I'm here?"

Willy shook his head mutely. He thought he must be sitting with a madwoman.

"And don't you go shaking your head neither or I'll go shaking this stick across it. I'm here, I tell you, because Ellen disobeyed me, her own father's sister that brought her up from an infant. Who was I to go meddling with children? Pests I always said they were. But they were Chaffeys, and for the sake of the Chaffeys I did it. I was never one to shirk my duty. And then what does she want to do but marry a man with a back street shop in *Ardwick*! In *Ardwick,* I'm telling you. Ellen, I said, you're a Chaffey; I didn't go rearing you to marry nobodies from Ardwick, you who've had every advantage: music lessons, a good table, and one of the best pews in the Joseph Street Wesleyan Chapel, and him with no more to offer than a house with two rooms up and two down and a shop in front. I'll take to my bed, Ellen, and never leave it if you bring this disgrace upon the Chaffeys. And I'll have no more to do with you. But

Ellen went her own way without a thought for me, and I've never seen her from that day to this. And what's more I've never left this bed neither. Still, you're a Chaffey all right, nothing of your father, whatever his name may be, in you. Not like that other lot of Kitty's who look like fat beef from Smithfield. I tell them so whenever they come, which is a great deal too often for my liking. They're after my money, that's why they're always here. How many are there of you?"

"There's me," whispered Willy, staring at her, horrified. "And George, he's ten."

"Is that all?"

"That's all."

"No girls?"

"No."

"There are two girls in Kitty's lot, wispy looking rats both of them. No Chaffey in *them*. I told Kitty to stop bringing them. But that husband of hers still brings the boy. He's the one that's going to inherit the property. It's down in the will, 'Stanley Sowter to have all my worldly goods'. It's a pity he don't look like you, though."

Willy had taken very little of this in. He was fidgeting on the end of the bed wondering when he could get a word in and ask to go. Sweat was pouring off him.

"I'd better be going. They'll be wondering at home."

"You tell them where you've been. Wait a bit though, how do you come to be here? I warrant that Sowter lot didn't tell you to come, did they?"

"They didn't tell me to come, no," said Willy hastily. Shuddering, he remembered the promises he had made to Stan down by the inky, foam-flecked water of the canal.

"*They* wouldn't tell you to come, not if I knows them. Why, all these years they wouldn't even tell me that Ellen had any sons. 'Don't you go talking about Ellen and her affairs, Auntie, you know it only upsets you'!" she mimicked. "They're afraid for the money, that's what it is, afraid their Stan won't get it." Then she pushed her head forward with greedy suspicion. "Did your folks go telling you to come and coax money out of me?"

"Of course they didn't," said Willy furiously. "They never say anything about you at home. It was only because . . ." Then he remembered Stan's threats again, "because the library was shut that I thought I'd walk around a bit and . . ." His voice trailed off guiltily.

"Well, when you get back you tell them who you've seen. You tell them all the property's going to Kitty's son. There's property and money too.

The property's this house, and the money I keep under me pillow. All in bank notes, it is, not gold. Gold jingles, might bring thieves. Not that thieves could get past them dogs. Did you hear the dogs downstairs? I likes to hear them tearing and thumping, it does me good. Open that bedroom door, I says to Hannah Raffetty sometimes. Open it and let me hear 'em at it, tearing and snarling and growling. Anyone who gets in among them, I'd like to see him when they've finished. So I sleeps easy on my money. And it's all going, lock, stock, and barrel to Kitty's son. You tell your mother that."

Willy nodded feverishly and raised himself off the bed. "I'm going now," he said in a faltering voice.

Miss Chaffey paid no attention. "I'm glad Ellen's got no girls, though," she said reflectively. "Girls is useless trash. Look at what they do to you. Look at Ellen, I say. Spared no trouble nor expense, I didn't. Piano lessons with a man as had a brass plate on his door, and then see what she did! Married into a back street in Ardwick!"

"I'm going!" shouted Willy.

"All right, you go. But you come back. I like to see a Chaffey. When are you coming back?"

"I don't know, there's school."

"You aren't at school the livelong year, are you? When do you have a holiday?"

"Not till Christmas."

"Christmas? When's Christmas? I don't know. The days come and go, I don't keep count. There's no school Saturdays, is there?"

"Not Saturdays, no," said Willy with the utmost reluctance, edging his way gingerly through the furniture but keeping a wary eye on Miss Chaffey.

"Then you come back to me next Saturday. Next Saturday, mind, and don't you forget." She crooked a bony finger at him and thumped her stick menacingly. "Morning, not afternoon. That boy of Kitty's and his father comes some afternoons."

"Next Saturday morning," promised Willy, hardly knowing what he was saying, and running now, bumping himself agonizingly against the corner of the massive sideboard near the door, but not stopping until he was safely outside on the landing. Then holding one hand to his side he limped downstairs. The old woman met him at the bottom.

"Well, you got out then."

"Yes."

"Was there any water in the jug?"

"I didn't see. She had a stick."

"She always has that stick. That's to call me up, when I chooses to go. But sometimes I don't choose. Sometimes it gets more than flesh and blood can bear. Fourteen years ago she took to her bed, and fourteen years I've been running about for her. She'll never leave that bed now, not till they carry her through this door in her coffin. Which won't be too soon for me, I'm telling you."

Willy was standing shivering by the front door. It was so cold in the hall that the old woman's breath was coming like smoke as she talked, and she kept her hand remorselessly on the door handle, barring the way out like a jailer. Behind a door down the hallway came menacing, savage growls.

"Them dogs. They know there's strangers about. They'll be tearing the place down soon. If it doesn't fall to bits first. It's rotten enough."

"I must *go*," said Willy wildly. "I didn't want to come and I want to go now."

"We all wants to go. Folks who can is lucky." Slowly the old woman drew the bolt back, undid the chain, and tugged at the door. "The damps gets into everything. They're in this dratted door, they're in my legs."

"I'll do it." Willy, with frenzied strength, pulled savagely at the handle. The swollen door gave way at last, and he staggered back. Recovering himself, he squeezed past the old woman, leaped down the steps and went running down the path. He could hear her voice behind him, but whether she was calling to him, shouting up to her mistress, or addressing the empty air, he did not want to know.

His mother was standing by the range when he got in, prodding with a fork in a saucepan. "The potatoes will be ten minutes yet—I waited to finish my ironing. See if you can find George. I sent him off to buy some chestnuts, but that was half an hour ago."

Willy stood staring by the door. A century seemed to have gone by since he last saw his mother, but she had noticed nothing. The kitchen was as friendly as ever, and full of comforting cooking smells, and she was talking placidly about dinner.

His mother glanced sharply over her shoulder. "There's nothing wrong, is there? Well, go and find George. There's a good boy. And take three-pence off the dresser in case he's forgotten the chestnuts. Father particularly said he'd like to roast some this evening."

Willy shut the door and went. He knew then that he was going to keep the doings of that morning to himself. He was not going to let the world of that mad old woman and her money and her dogs seep into the warm kitchen where the four of them would be sitting that evening, roasting chestnuts in the ash pan of the range, and him and George kneeling on the coconut mat with their heads close together, trying to peel off the red-hot skins.

But the thought that he would have to go back to High Street himself poisoned everything. She would send old Hannah Raffetty for him if he did not. All the following week he brooded about it, a monstrous nightmare that he could not escape.

Nor did the darkness of a Manchester November help: the dingy yellowness, the smell of smoke in the air, the lights on at school all day, the return home through a damp twilight, over pavements that gleamed wet and black. When Saturday came, the dampness had turned to rain, a steady light rain from a heavy, gray sky. It was his turn to sieve the cinders and chop the firewood, and when he had done it he scrambled into his overcoat, and wound his muffler around his neck. His mother came out of the scullery while he dressed himself.

"It's not the day for being out, you with that cold and your weak chest. Why don't you come into the kitchen and sit by the fire? I haven't that much baking to do today."

"I thought I might go to the library."

"That Mr. Church of yours didn't know what

he'd started when he put you on to the library. Well, mind you wrap up well, then, and don't stay out long."

He ran down the wet street out to Oxford Street, and then trotted down the long road that led south out of Manchester. His breath came sobbingly and words pounded around his brain. He wasn't going to let that old woman say all the things she liked about his father and Ardwick and his shop. His father was far better than Uncle Harold, he'd tell her that straight out; she could take it or leave it.

But by the time he turned down High Street he was very weary, so weary that he seemed to have lost the power even to think about what lay ahead. He dragged himself up the path of Laurel Villas, and hammered weakly on the door with his fist; there seemed no other way of calling anybody's attention. There was the sound of feet shuffling along the floor inside, of the chain being lifted, of the door being pulled. Then old Hannah Raffetty peered at him. He stared at her mutely, wondering if she had ever left the hall since last week. Certainly the bonnet did not seem to have left her head, it looked more battered than ever, her clothes more bedraggled.

"She seed you coming, she's been thumping and screeching at me like something crazed. She says you're her nephew. Is that right?"

"Yes, I suppose so."

The old woman peered at him disbelievingly. "You're not like that other lot that comes on Saturday afternoons. Why didn't you come before, then?"

"I didn't know anything about her. Nobody told me about her."

"Oh, you're one of the lot as she won't see. The lot that made her take to her bed. That was a fine thing you did. Making her take to her bed like that and use *me* for her legs!"

Willy stared at her blankly. "It wasn't me that did it. I didn't know about it. Not till last week, I didn't."

"And now as you know you'll be hanging around for the pickings, I daresay."

"Pickings?" Willy asked weakly. His head felt light and dizzy, he was finding it difficult to follow.

"What them two others are after. That boy and his father. Comes here most Saturday afternoons they do, and talk sweet to her and hope as they'll get all the money. Oh there's money right enough though she won't let no one see it. Keeps it under her pillow. Piles of it, but she's as close-fisted with it as . . ." Hannah Raffetty searched around for a word strong enough, but words failed her, and she shook her head.

At this moment a thunderous pounding on the floor above startled them both. "He's there, and you're keeping him from me, Hannah Raffetty. You let go of him and let him come up here. He's my flesh and blood and not yours." The voice and the thumping set the dogs barking in a frenzy, and sent stabs of pain through Willy's head.

"We'll have the whole house falling to bits about us what with her and them dogs. Dear knows it's rotten enough. Go on, you go up to her. I've took care not to have that jug of hers filled, so you won't need to be thinking about it."

Willy dragged himself up the stairs. Miss Chaffey was crouching forward on the bed, expectant.

"So you've come. Taken your time, haven't you? I could hear you talking to Hannah Raffetty, that lazy good-for-nothing. You come and sit down and let me look at you. I like looking at a Chaffey. Chaffeys have got bones. You can't see any bones on that Sowter lot. I'd like to take a knife to them and hack some of the flesh off."

Willy picked his way through the furniture. He did not seem able to see straight, and the corners came up and hit him as though they were lying in wait.

"Now then, sit down and talk to me," commanded Miss Chaffey.

He stared at her aghast, at her wrinkled and hollow face, and the hairs that straggled out under the dirty cap.

"Well, you aren't saying much. Those Sowters have more to say."

Willy ran his tongue around his dry lips, and wiped the back of his hand over his forehead. All the angry words he had prepared had vanished, he groped for them, but his brain felt empty and dark.

"Do you like your cousin Stanley?"

"No."

"And your uncle Harold, what about him?"

"I don't like him neither."

"Why not? Boys ought to like their cousins and their uncles."

"Uncle Harold is a fat lout." To his astonishment Willy heard his own voice speaking these strange words, and listened with curiosity to know what it would say next. "And so is Stan. I'd like to kick Stan, but I'd like to kick Uncle Harold harder."

There came a sort of shriek from the bed and Miss Chaffey fell back on her pillows. Frightened by what he had said, Willy stared at her. Her eyes were closed and she was gasping and panting.

"I didn't mean . . ." he muttered. But then he stopped because he had no idea what it was he didn't mean.

Miss Chaffey opened her eyes and leaned forward on an elbow. "Don't you go taking that back because I'm not having it. Fourteen years and I haven't laughed till you came. Go on. Say it again."

Willy stared at her with hot, frightened eyes. He backed away, flattening himself against the foot of the bed.

"Go on, I tell you. Say it again, 'Uncle Harold is a fat lout . . .' "

"I'd like to kick him," gabbled Willy, clutching the rails behind him and twisting sweaty hands around them. "And Stan too."

"You get Hannah Raffetty." Miss Chaffey pointed a lean finger at him. "You tell her I want my will. I'm going to alter it. Oh, yes, I am. Those Sowters aren't going to get my money. Oh, no, they aren't. It's you who's going to get it, you who's made me laugh for the first time in fourteen years."

· 9 ·

THE DOCTOR'S OPINION

How he got home, Willy never knew. He had no clear recollection even of getting out of the room. He didn't see Hannah Raffetty on the way down, or if he did, he did not remember. He did remember pulling at the swollen door in a frenzy, and how he caught his foot on the threshold as he tried to escape, and crashed down the steps.

He must have fallen heavily because his mother later exclaimed with horror at the oozing blood on his legs as she peeled his stockings from him. But at the time he felt no pain; he picked himself up and pelted down the street, forgetting in his terror that neither of the two old women at Laurel Villas could possibly run after him.

Then there was a blank in his memory, and he

was back in the kitchen in Audley Street, leaning
against the door post and watching his mother
stooping by the oven door of the range. She
turned to ask him if he knew where George was,
and his legs crumpled as if they had been paper.
Instead of standing, he was sitting on the floor,
leaning against the wall.

With a little scream, his mother dropped a baking pan on the floor. Through a muzzy haze he
heard the clatter. She came over to him and tried
to get him to his feet but he felt like the rag doll
that he mistily remembered Lily had once possessed, all limp and sagging.

Then his father came, and between them he was
hauled up to bed. He remembered the hot bricks
wrapped in flannel that were put to his icy feet,
and how George with a frightened face, seemed
always to be coming with a new one and taking
away the old. A fire was lit in the tiny grate—
something he never remembered before—and
the red light danced on his hot, aching eyes, till he
had to shut them.

A long time went by in which he was aware of
nothing except that his chest seemed full of red-
hot knives. He was raging with thirst, but to
stretch out an arm for the mug by his bed was too
much effort. Sometimes his mother would be

there holding him up and letting him drink. Sometimes she would be rubbing his chest with camphor out of a dark blue bottle, or giving him medicine from a tablespoon which she held against his shaking lips. Sometimes he would be on fire and want to throw off all the bedclothes. Sometimes he would be shivering so much that the whole bed shook and the medicine would spill down his nightshirt, and trickle cold on his skin.

And there would be frightful dreams, dreams about old women screaming at him, about shadowy dogs lurking in corners ready to leap at his throat out of the darkness, and of a coffin being carried out of the shop past the upturned counter, and he was in that coffin suffocating.

How long all this lasted he had no idea. He knew there was a time when he seemed to come out from a long tunnel where nightmares, thirst, and discomfort had never left him. He just felt very weak now. All he wanted to do was stare at the ceiling. He didn't want to talk to anybody, it was an effort to tell them even that he felt better, or to raise his shoulders off the pillow to swallow the beef tea that his mother spooned into his mouth.

He timed the day by the noises around him, which seemed to belong to an infinitely remote life. He could not imagine that he would ever take part in it again. First there would be the sound of heavy cart wheels stopping outside the house, and thuds that rattled the shop door. This was the newspapers arriving for the shop. Then the wheels and the clopping of the horse again, retreating into the distance. Soon after this, sharp ears could detect the knocker-up at the far end of the street, rattling on the window, pausing, calling, marching on.

Inside, the house would begin to stir. First, the creaking of the bed in the next room as his father got up, his footsteps on the stairs, the distant sound of the shovel scraping as he cleared out the range, of water clanging into the kettle. More thumping, more creaking as his mother got up. A banging on the door to wake George who was back sleeping with Willy now. Then George, muttering and yawning, would be pulling on his clothes in the darkness, stumbling out of the room and down the stairs.

The sound of the buzzer was not far off now. Tense, Willy would lie dreading that gathering howl. Then the rush and clatter of footsteps in the street, and a voice calling here and there to another. Silence, then the banging of doors and the patter of feet as the children left for school. A bit later and doors would open again and he could hear scrubbing brushes and the scrape of women stoning their steps and their windowsills, and the occasional wail of a small child who got slapped for getting in his mother's way. Long silence now, before the children's feet came running home to dinner. Then, when they had gone back, and the street and the house were at their stillest, his mother would come up and sit with him for an hour or so, bringing her mending or her knitting, and sitting on his bed. This was the best time of the day, and the worst was when she lit the gas and went downstairs to prepare for a comfortable evening in the warmth of the kitchen from which he was excluded.

By the time he got downstairs it was nearly Christmas, and he found to his horror that he didn't mind whether it was Christmas or not. It had never occurred to him that it was possible not to be excited about Christmas, and yet here he was now, sitting limply by the range, watching his mother chopping raisins, taking the candied sugar from the peel, skinning almonds, and he did not even want to stir the pudding. His mother had put off making the pudding until he was well, and as far as he was concerned, she might just as well have done it at her usual time.

Decorating the shop window was another great

Christmas ritual. He and George were usually clamoring to begin, discussing their ideas for it, and reporting how Scroggins had done it down Grosvenor Street, and how poverty-struck his had looked. But this year he didn't care.

George rushed in one evening. "Father says we can decorate tomorrow, and he's laid on a lot of stuff that looks like snow, and some lanterns— colored paper ones."

"You do it," said Willy. "I don't want to."

When he heard himself say this he thought that there was no hope left. If he didn't want to decorate the shop window, then he could hardly enjoy Christmas Day itself.

Nor did he. Part of the trouble was that he had no presents to give anybody, and everybody had been very generous in what they gave him. George had spent more than he could afford, so that he had little left for his parents. He had bought him a clasp knife with two blades, a corkscrew, and an implement for digging stones out of horses' hooves. His mother, who usually gave a joint present with his father, bought him a black cap with ear flaps, lined with tartan, and his father produced *The Boyhoods of Famous Men*, the first book he had ever given him; it must have meant a journey right into Manchester to get it.

He stood proudly by while Willy unwrapped it. It was very handsome, with gilt lettering on the back and pictures inside. Willy dutifully turned over the pages and thanked his father.

"That's a book you'll treasure all your life, Willy," said his mother. "You keep it nice, mind."

"And you'll look at it when you're a great man yourself, Willy," said his father, "and you'll say to yourself that that and Smiles first set you on the road. Don't you like it then? I went all the way to Sherratt and Hughes for it. It's not the sort of book you can get at any street corner."

"Don't fret the lad," put in his mother hastily. "He's still feeling low, and there's been a lot of excitement today to tire him out."

It was worse on Boxing Day. Traditionally, the Overs family all went to eat a tea of cold fowl and ham and mince pies with the Sowters the day after Christmas. But in view of Willy's illness, the Sowters were all coming over to Ardwick this year. He had not seen any of them since that day in November just after the piano arrived. When they all crowded into the parlor where he was sitting with his knees wrapped up in an invalidish way, he thought peevishly how big Uncle Harold and Stan were. Just like the prize oxen whose pictures you saw in the *Evening News* around Christmas time.

And it was then that he remembered Miss Chaffey. "Fat beef from Smithfield," she had called them. He could hear her voice now. Until this moment he had not given a thought to those visits to Laurel Villas. The fever seemed to have wiped them clean out of his mind. But now it all came surging back. What had become of her? Had she been after him, sending Hannah Raffetty to see why he had not been back? What had he said when he was ill? Did his parents know about her? He stared around the room wildly; he could hardly sit still in his agitation.

"He's still not looking well," his Aunt Kitty was saying, peering at him with her head on one side. "Very poorly he looks, I'd say. You take care of him, Ellen. There's plenty as goes into a decline after a fever like that. Did you have a doctor see him?"

"Well, I might have thought of it if it'd gone on much longer. I used more medicine on him than I've ever used in my life. I had to send out three times for more. And a whole bottle of camphor."

"He always was a puny-looking lad," said Auntie Kitty, pursing her lips and slowly taking off her cape. "Not like our Stan, I'm thankful to say. Stan takes after his Pa. There's breadth there."

"Well, I'd rather look puny than look like a fat

ox. Him and his bulging eyes!" said Willy in a high squeaking voice, and burst into tears.

Consternation clouded every face in the room, especially as Willy found himself quite unable to stop crying. Tears poured down his face, his chest heaved, his breath came in gasps. His parents looked at him uneasily, and then at each other. Auntie Kitty nodded her head meaningly, and exchanged glances with Uncle Harold. Stan sniggered, and Dolly and Lily looked as though they were going to cry too.

"He's off his food and a bit low," said his mother. "Now, if you'll all be sitting down I'll make the tea and Alfred can carve the fowl."

But all through tea the tears rolled down Willy's face. He brushed them aside furiously with the back of his hand, but he could not stop them. His parents gave him furtive glances, Auntie Kitty looked pitying, and Uncle Harold talked loudly, so loudly that the walls seemed to shake and Willy's head reeled.

"I like lads that have got go," he kept saying. "When I take on a boy, first I see whether he can look me straight in the eyes. If he don't, then he's out. Then I see whether he's got go, can stand up to a man and not cringe like a girl. I like a lad that's a thruster. Young Stan here'll be a thruster. That boy of yours needs a tonic. Give him a bit of iron;

his blood's too thin, that's what it is. Look how he picks at his food. No child of mine's allowed to pick at their food. Eh Dolly, eh Lily? I make 'em eat up all right."

And his aunt's last words to his mother as she left the parlor were, "I think you ought to let that boy see a doctor, Ellen, I do really. Look, he's crying still. You take him before he gets into a decline."

When his parents came back from seeing the Sowters off, they were talking in low voices. His mother came up to his chair. "Is there anything hurting you, Willy, love? Is your head hurting you again?"

"There's nothing wrong. It's just I can't stop." But he could hardly speak, his breath was coming in such spasms. "Mother, has there been anybody here asking after me? Any old women or that? Somebody who said I hadn't been to see her like I ought?" His tears became more violent and he collapsed again into breathless sobs.

"Any old women?" said his mother amazed. "What is the lad talking of? There's plenty who've been into the shop asking after you, and bringing you jelly and this and that. But I've told you all about them. You haven't got the fever again, have you?" She pressed the back of her hand anxiously to his forehead.

"Kitty's right," said his father with resolution. "That boy ought to see a doctor. Crying like that's not natural, not in a boy."

"It's only just that he's weak," pleaded his mother, "and he wouldn't have gone on so if Kitty and Harold hadn't talked to him like that. He's picking up, aren't you, Willy?"

"He's been weak for too long. You take him to the doctor on Monday."

To go to the doctor was a very grave step, Willy knew that, and when he heard his father's firm voice, his tears, which had begun to stop, started afresh. It turned out that his mother was not going to take him to the Independent Dispensary and Surgery in Grosvenor Street, the one that had painted on its window ADVICE AND MEDICINE 6D. VISIT AND MEDICINE IS 6D. This was where everybody in Audley Street usually went if they felt that illness had got out of hand and alarming.

Mr. Overs said firmly that this was not good enough, and if it came to the point of consulting a doctor, he was going to have a chap with a brass plate on his door and letters after his name. There was Dr. Parker in Ardwick Green; that was where Willy must be taken, and he'd be hanged if he cared how much he had to pay.

And thus it came about that Willy went out for the first time in weeks, on legs that seemed to have telescoped and to be somewhere miles below the rest of him. He was muffled in layers and layers of clothes, so that it was difficult to bend at any point. He wore, in addition to a woolen scarf tied around his head, the black cap with earflaps that his mother had given him. His mother held his arm, and slowly they crept down to Grosvenor Street, turned right at Downing Street, and made their way around Ardwick Green to the far side.

The doctor's house was a tall one with railings in front, and a flight of steps which Willy by this time felt almost too weary to climb. The doctor was a lean, bony man with a bald, shiny head. He made Willy peel off his layers of clothes (it was like taking the skins off an onion), and lie shivering on an icy leather couch. Then he prodded and poked him, and Willy gasped at the cold touch of those white bony fingers. He listened to Willy's chest with an instrument that was even colder. Then he allowed him to dress.

There was nothing wrong with him, it seemed, that a good iron tonic could not put right. "Parrish's Food?" said his mother, timidly, twisting the handles of her bag.

Yes, Parrish's Food would do very well. And the boy needed taking out of himself, a short holiday by the sea, a change of air perhaps? It wouldn't be long before the young man was set on his feet again. And he patted Willy on the shoulder. The fee for consultation was seven shillings and six-pence, thank you very much.

Mrs. Overs contained herself until they had descended the steps, and then her outraged horror could no longer be held back.

"Seven shillings and sixpence! Did you ever hear the like for sheer, rank wickedness! Half a crown I'd have thought dear, but I would have paid without saying much seeing he's a man with letters after his name, and they're not like peas on the ground. Five shillings would have been a scandal and daylight robbery. But seven and sixpence! And not even a bottle of medicine at the end of it, and me having to put Parrish's Food in his mind! I never could have believed that such barefaced impudence could be possible!"

And she repeated this and very much more to Mr. Overs when she got back to the shop. "Well, there's one piece of advice we're going to follow whatever it costs us. Willy has got to be taken out of himself. I want to know that we've got something out of that seven and sixpence." And she made her way angrily into the kitchen.

"We'll do something about it, never you mind, Willy lad," said his father. "It won't be a seaside holiday. But we'll talk it out, your mother and me, and see what we can do."

· IO ·

TAKING WILLY OUT
OF HIMSELF

What Mr. Overs did do was the talk of Audley Street for weeks. It was nothing less
than a tandem bicycle, which nobody in that part
of Ardwick had ever set eyes on except in pictures.
He had gone off for it one Sunday afternoon.
They all knew there was to be a big surprise; he
had talked of it gloatingly for days. It was to be a
surprise bigger than anything they had ever
known, he told them, just let them wait. This
would make Mrs. Jericho sit up, this would make
the eyes of the Sowters pop more than nature
made them.

"Alfred!" said Mrs. Overs warningly, and then
said that she hoped it was respectable, what he had
in mind. She didn't want the neighbors talking,
and if they talked it might affect trade.

Mr. Overs had slapped his leg and assured them all that what he had in mind was quite respectable. It might make folk sit up a bit, but where was the harm in that. And it would be the making of Willy. He would tell them no more, except that they were to be in the front of the house around four o'clock that Sunday afternoon and then they would know everything.

As four o'clock approached, George went up to the front bedroom. Willy wasn't allowed up there. Although he was back at school, he was still being watched very carefully by his mother, and made to take Parrish's Food night and morning, and keep warm and out of drafts. He sat in the kitchen with the door slightly open. He was not as excited as George; his spirits still had not fully revived; but he was fidgety and couldn't settle into anything.

Then at the same time as Willy seemed to hear a faint tinkling like a bell from the street, George came crashing downstairs, poked his head into the kitchen and shouted, "It's a bicycle! The longest one you've ever seen, it's like one of them sausage dogs!"

They all went pounding up the passage, through the parlor, through the shop, and stood at the door marveling. There was Mr. Overs, and there, propped against the wall was this monster of a bicycle with two high handlebars and two

seats, and everybody in the houses opposite standing at their front doors gaping.

"You go back in this minute, Willy, and put on
your muffler and your overcoat," ordered Mrs.
Overs. "You didn't ride that through the street,
Alfred?" she said scandalized. "Not on a Sunday!"

"Well, I rode a bit of the way, since I had to bring
it from Moss Side. But not after I got to Oxford
Road. It's a champion, right enough. Those pedals going around with your feet on them! Took me
back to being a boy, when we used to ride the bike
Jo Bagnall's father had in his shop. It'll be the
making of our Willy. Just wait till we hoist him
onto that seat. We'll have him pedaling away getting all the fresh air and change that that doctor
ordered!"

But when Willy reappeared with his coat on and
his muffler wound about him, his mother would
not hear of him trying the bicycle. She had never
heard of such a thing on a Sunday, she said. What
would all the neighbors think, especially that lot
on the other side who knew no better. If it wasn't
light enough on weekdays to try it after the shop
had shut, why, they would have to wait until next
Saturday, that was all. It wouldn't run away.

In the end Willy was allowed to sit on the seat,
when Mr. Overs had brought the tandem around
to the yard at the back. It was almost as long as the

yard, so there was no question of riding it there. But Willy and his father mounted and practiced putting their feet on the pedals and whirling them around backward while they supported themselves against the wall. Then George had a turn too.

"Such rides we'll have, boys!" said Mr. Overs, dismounting. "All over the place seeing the sights, Belle Vue, Alexandra Park, and further off— Stockport and Salford. I've planned it all. All work and no play makes Jack a dull boy. So now that business is good I'm going to take on that young Huggins from Crown Street. He's new married and like to be a family man soon, and he said he'd be glad of a few extra shillings now and again. So he'll come to look after the shop some Saturday afternoon, and you and me, Willy, we'll go for spins around the place. And when Willy's himself again, then it'll be George's turn."

It took a few weeks before Willy was fit to undertake a proper ride. The new skill was quite difficult to acquire. You had to take care to get your pedals moving at the same pace as the person in front of you. If your foot slipped, then the sharp iron of the pedal was liable to come up and hit you an agonizing blow on the shin, which would make you lurch and throw out the balance of the other rider.

Up and down Audley Street they practiced on

Saturdays, with the people on the respectable side
peering at them from behind their curtains, and
the people on the other side quite openly standing
on the street and shouting after them. Mr. Overs
used to wave a cheerful hand, but Willy felt self-
conscious.

All the same, whether it was Parrish's Food, or
his mother's care, or the bicycling, he was much
better. He was more cheerful, he had strength in
his legs again, and he had begun to enjoy things.
He was enjoying school again. He had found little
difficulty in catching up after his long absence; in
fact, Mr. Church was teaching him more advanced
geometry, and giving him lists of books to borrow
from the free library. And the weather was good.
For January it was a miracle—sunny mild days
that felt like spring. People talked of the winter
being over, and said how lucky they were to have
escaped so lightly.

Then one Saturday at breakfast Mr. Overs
announced his plans. "Willy has got the trick of it
at last. So I tell you what you and me are going to
do this afternoon, Willy. We're going over to Trafford, and give them the shock of their lives at
Cromwell Villas. See what happens to their eyes,
eh?"

"It's first Sunday tomorrow," said Mrs. Overs
doubtfully. "We'll be seeing them there anyway."

"That's just what I have in mind," said Mr. Overs boisterously. "They won't believe it if we just tell them about the machine. They need to see us on it before they realize that we've got what they haven't. And I'd like Harold to know that I can take a Saturday afternoon off the same as him."

Willy wore his cap with the earflaps for the occasion, and they were seen off by Mrs. Overs, George, a motley crowd of boys from the other side of the road, and a few idlers who happened to be hanging around.

"We'll be a long time, lads," said Mr. Overs boisterously. "So don't waste your afternoon waiting for us to come back."

Down into Grosvenor Street they went, and up Oxford Street toward the city. Then they swung down Bridgewater Street and into Chester Road. It was hard work, but very satisfying to feel both pedals moving together and the city streets disappearing fast under their wheels.

"All right there?" Mr. Overs called back over his shoulder from time to time. "My word, but those Sowters are in for a surprise. I feel quite sorry for them, that I do."

Willy, behind, with his eyes fixed on his father's back, rather wished they had not undertaken this jaunt. He did not feel very confident that the

Overs were going to come out on top. The Sowters took a lot of beating, he knew that.

He felt even more apprehensive when they reached Cromwell Villas. His father, with a fine air of bravado, settled the tandem by the curb directly opposite the gate of the Sowters' house, a procedure which took some time. Then he pushed open the gate and strode up the path. Willy stood lurking behind as his father gave a thundering knock on the door. It seemed a long time before anybody came. His father took off his glove, and twirled his mustache end jauntily, and then reached out for another knock. He had indeed just grasped the knocker when the door was opened. The knocker fell with a crash, and Lily's pale, frightened face peeped around the door.

"Why, hullo, Lily," said Mr. Overs in a loud, hearty voice. "Your Pa in?"

"Well, yes, he's in," faltered Lily, giving a nervous look over her shoulder and making no attempt to open the door wider.

"Then let's see him. We've got something to show you all, Willy and me. Why, come on, lass, why don't you go and fetch him, eh?"

Lily's face got longer and her eyes got bigger and she hesitated. "Oh, please, Uncle Alf, I dursen't. Not when he's napping under his pocket handkerchief."

But Uncle Harold was no longer under his pocket handkerchief, it seemed. A door down the passage was flung open angrily, and there was the sound of heavy feet. "What's all this row? Didn't I tell you children there'd got to be hush! Call this hush, all this banging and stamping and roaring! I'll thrash hush into you before I've finished."

Lily disappeared with a frightened squeak. "Oh, Pa," they could hear her bleating. "It's Uncle Alf and Willy, and they says they wants to see you particular."

"Uncle Alf, my fanny," said Mr. Sowter contemptuously. "It's tomorrow that's first Sunday, not today. You must have gone clean out of your wits. Not that you ever had any." The door was now wrenched sharply open, and there stood Uncle Harold. He had no collar on, there were down-at-heel slippers on his feet, and a large spotted handkerchief in his hand. His face was flushed and angry.

"Oh, so it is you, Alf. The girl said it was but I told her she was mistook. Seems she was right after all. Made a mistake, haven't you? It's tomorrow you was coming."

All this had taken a lot of the jauntiness out of Mr. Overs. He was now fingering his mustache nervously rather than twirling it, and his shoulders drooped a little.

"Oh, yes, it's first Sunday tomorrow, right enough. But Willy and me came over to show you a thing we'd just bought. Not the kind of thing you can bring out on a Sunday. It's here." He waved a nonchalant hand at the gate.

Mr. Sowter stared at the long machine outside, with its two sets of handlebars and seats. His eyes bulged and his nostrils swelled. The Overs stood there anxiously waiting for his comment.

"Well, all I can say is, Alf, you must have gone out of your mind. How much did you pay for that tomfool thing?"

"It was five pounds from a chap I knew down in Moss Side. Good as new, it was."

"It'd have to be, at that price. Getting a bit reckless, aren't you? Whatever did you want to go throwing hard-earned cash after a thing like that for?"

Mr. Overs squared his shoulders and put on a voice that tried to ring with confidence. "Dr. Parker, the one in Ardwick Green with a brass plate outside his door, said as how our Willy needed a change, and I thought to myself that this was no time of the year for the seaside and that kind of trash. So how about a bit of fresh air, I said to myself. One of my customers told me about this machine which one of his friends had for the asking, so down I went to get it. Paid the chap cash and came home with it. Willy and I thought that before we set off for any little jaunts we'd show you and Stan and the girls what a bicycle made for two looked like."

"Stan, Lily, Dolly!" bellowed Mr. Sowter, "your uncle's here with a bicycle made for two, he says. Come on, can't you, are you going to keep me propping this door open all day on a Saturday afternoon?"

There was a sound of scuffling feet in the hall, and then Stan pushed his way past his father, and stood staring at the Overs. Behind him, Lily and Dolly sidled out and blinked like startled guinea pigs.

"Go on," shouted Mr. Sowter, "go and look at it, and then I can shut this door and get on with my nap."

"Come along, girls," said Mr. Overs, "I warrant you've never seen one like this. You just come and see."

"We seed them in Alexandra Park," piped Lily.

"There's ladies as ride them sometimes, behind a gentleman," put in Dolly. "They wear bloomers. Ma says it isn't respectable, and Pa says he'll tan our backsides afore we do it."

But they went down the path with Mr. Overs to look. Stan was left staring at Willy.

"When they've had their look you get them in and shut that door *quietly*," said Mr. Sowter. "Else it'll be the worst for you. And not a squeak or a pipe out of you until teatime, do you hear?"

When Uncle Harold's steps had retreated down the hall Stan pulled the door until it was nearly shut. Heavily he came down the steps, advanced toward Willy, and stared at him. Daunted, Willy moved back a pace or two.

"I've been wanting to see you," said Stan ominously. "You know what about, don't you?"

Willy shook his head. He looked apprehensively over his shoulder at the group standing on the pavement around the tandem.

"It's about what I told you down by the canal. What I said you wasn't to tell to no one. Well, who've you been a telling?"

"Father knows that I know a bit," whispered Willy. "But that's not because I told him. He guessed, honest he did. But he's forgot all about it now, I'm sure of it. He only spoke of it once, then he bought a piano for Mother and forgot about the other."

Stan seized Willy by the fleshy part of the arm, and gripped until he gave a little shriek of pain. "There's somebody been talking to the old lady, I'm sure of it. She's acting very queer, talking about Chaffeys all of a sudden, and those who do look like Chaffeys and those who don't. You been there?" He dug his nails savagely into Willy's arm.

"I didn't want to go. She called me in, said I looked like a Chaffey, she knew me. I wish I'd never seen her. I don't want to go there ever again."

"Well then, don't. Just you keep your long nose out of other people's affairs."

"She's not been asking after me, then?"

"Asking after you! You've got brass, thinking anybody'd ask after *you*, little Willy Overs of Ardwick!"

"It was just that she seemed so keen, like, before Christmas," said Willy defiantly.

"She's not keen now and won't never be again, so just you keep out of it, see. You keep yourself in dirty old Ardwick, and then you won't go far wrong."

At this point Mr. Overs came back through the gate, with Lily and Dolly trailing behind. "You seen it, Stan? Come and have a look before we take to the road again."

Giving Willy a last threatening scowl, Stan slouched off to the gate, stared, grunted, and turned away.

"Maybe you and Willy'll be doing a little spin

together one day," said Mr. Overs cheerfully. "If there's any place around about you fancy seeing."

Stan muttered words to the effect that he would know better than sit perched up there gawping at Willy's backside. Only Willy caught the drift of this, and Mr. Overs was still smiling when he and Willy mounted and pushed themselves off. But it was not a very confident smile.

· I I ·

THE LADDER APPROACHES

Just as Mrs. Overs had said that it made her flesh creep to think of that fight in the streets between George and Stan, so Willy's flesh crept now. The Sowters between them had made him and his father look like idiots, and he could hardly bear to mount on that freak of a machine and pedal off on it knowing that Stan's scornful eyes were fixed on their retreating backs. Everything about it seemed ridiculous—the way their feet twirled around like one; him perched up there with his face crammed into his father's back. Not a word would he utter on the homeward journey: he pretended that the wind was blowing his father's words past him and that he could not hear.

Nor did it end with that trip to Trafford. He wouldn't look at his father; he kept his head down and answered in a surly way when he was spoken to. Mr. Overs gave up trying to get him interested in the tandem and its affairs, and turned to George instead.

George was more than willing. He was almost as devoted to the machine as Mr. Overs himself— and Mr. Overs doted on it like a mother with her firstborn. Even in the dinner hour he used to go out into the yard and lift off the tarpaulins that covered it as it leaned against the whitewashed wall, and just stand and gaze. Mr. Huggins, a tall gangly young man with drooping shoulders, came in regularly now on Saturday afternoons and looked after the shop while Mr. Overs looked after the tandem and its well-being. George stood beside him, absorbed, handing him the tools and the oily rags and the metal polish, and his father cleaned, adjusted, tightened up screws. Willy took care to be well out of the way, and when George came in to ask him that Father wanted to know, did he want to go for a ride, he was always absorbed in a book, or hammering away at the piano. No, he didn't want to go out, George could go if he wanted. So Saturday after Saturday through those winter months George and Mr. Overs bowled around the city streets and came back with cold hands and a high color to boast over tea about how well the tandem was going and the sights they had seen.

"Pity you didn't come, Willy," his father would say, "you'd have enjoyed yourself. You take care you don't read your eyes out. There's a great deal more to life than books, as I'm always telling you."

But Willy, with his eyes fixed on his plate, would only mumble excuses, and his mother would hastily break in. "Don't tease the lad. It's no weather for him to be out on a bicycle. Wait till the spring comes, then he'll come with you."

Mild, springlike weather came with the beginning of March, but no desire to mount the tandem possessed Willy. It seemed a long time, too, since he had wanted to do anything with his father. They hardly ever spoke to each other these days. There was a feeling of constraint and unease, and the only time he was really happy was when he was at school.

One Friday evening he was standing morosely in the yard. It was just growing dark; the sky was a cold, clear blue, with the evening star gleaming in it. A faint breeze ruffled his hair, and somewhere in the distance a blackbird was singing among the chimney pots. He remembered the happiness of that April morning six years before when he had run away to the park and had knelt in the sun pick-

ing daffodils, and he suddenly felt savage with
rebellion. He hated Ardwick, *"Ardwick!"* he muttered with compressed lips and saw in his mind
those tight little black houses squeezed together,
each puffing up its column of yellow-gray smoke,
and the people who lived in them peering out
through their curtains at his father making a sight
of himself on his tandem. Then as he said it, he
heard the hoarse old voice that had terrified him
in November, just before he was ill.

Miss Chaffey—she had faded from his mind as
if she was just one of his feverish dreams. But she
was real enough, and she hated Ardwick. That
made two of them. And he almost wanted, in the
strength of his feeling, to go and tell her so. He'd
been a fool to let himself get worked up into such a
fright, it must have been because he was getting ill.
He wouldn't be frightened now, he was Chaffey
same as her, more Chaffey than Overs, he reck-
oned.

Absorbed in his seething discontent, he didn't
hear his father coming down the steps into the
yard, and he jumped like a scalded cat when Mr.
Overs spoke to him.

"Well, Willy, coming out for a spin tomorrow?
Looks as though we're settled in for a fine spell."

"Where to?" muttered Willy with lowered head.

"I thought Rochdale. It's quite a way, but the machine's going like a bird, it'll take us there light as a feather."

"What's in Rochdale?" said Willy sulkily.

"Why you've heard me talk about it often enough. It's where the Co-operative Movement started. It's a fine Lancashire town."

"Mills!" said Willy with hatred. "And chimneys."

"There will be some I daresay. But it's the ride we go for, isn't it? That's why we bought the bike, to get you out and about. Five pounds it cost, but I didn't grudge it, not to get you like yourself again. And now you won't look at it. I don't know what's come over you these days, Willy. It used to be a real treat to be with you, and now look at you—can't even speak civil. What's wrong, Willy?" And Mr. Overs came up and put a hand on Willy's shoulder.

But Willy shook it off. "There are enough mills here, aren't there, without going all the way to Rochdale to see them?" he shouted. He could feel the anger rushing up into his head, and the passionate words surging inside him. "I never asked for that tandem. You and George go and make fools of yourself on it if you want to!" And on shaking legs he ran into the house, slamming the back door so that the whole house trembled.

If the past few weeks had been constrained

and uneasy, they were joyful compared to that evening. Willy wouldn't eat—he couldn't have if he had wanted to, his throat felt so tight. He just pushed his plate away and shook his head dumbly when his mother started her anxious inquiries.

"Stop pampering the lad," shouted his father. "There's nothing wrong with him except wicked bad temper. If he won't eat, let him starve. He's been spoiled for too long, that's his trouble—that and all his reading and fiddling about with the piano. The sooner he's finished with school and all that nonsense the better, I say. You can all be thankful that next term's his last. A taste of working for his living will bring him to his senses."

After that, nobody said anything, and Willy went up to bed as soon as tea was over and pretended to be asleep when George arrived an hour later. Saturday was passed in silence too. Mr. Overs took George off on a ride so far afield that they were to have tea out at a teashop before they came back. In their absence, Mrs. Overs tried to tempt Willy out of his sullen silence by cooking him pancakes with jam inside, and when he ate only half of one, she said that it was Parrish's Food that he needed. He still hadn't got his strength back after the fever. But Willy just shook his head. He felt locked in his misery, and no amount of kindness helped.

He was in bed by the time his father and George returned, but not asleep—he had only gone there to get out of their way, and he heard their voices in the passage downstairs. His father was fully restored to his usual cheerful loud spirits.

"What, gone to bed already? What's wrong with the lad?"

His mother must have said something about him working hard at his lessons, for Mr. Overs went on, "Lessons! Lessons of life, that's what young Willy wants, not school learning. The sooner he gets fixed up with some real work, the sooner he'll be back to himself. I'll speak to Mr. Ramsbottom the next time I see him. It's none too soon to be thinking about the lad's future. Well, his tantrums lost him a right good trip, eh George? Ten miles an hour we was averaging, what do you think of that? Could have gone twice as far, if it hadn't been for the getting back. Yes, I'll have a word with Mr. Ramsbottom. A week or two at the Northern Star, and our Willy will be begging to come out on our Saturday trips."

The word with Mr. Ramsbottom came sooner than even Mr. Overs expected. The next day being Sunday, they went to chapel, as they always did, in Grosvenor Street, though there was little that Willy took in that day. After chapel it was the family habit to go for a short walk. The roast was already in the oven, the potatoes baking under it, and unless the weather was particularly bad they used to go for a stroll around the streets to work up an appetite for the business ahead, as Mr. Overs put it.

"Well now, Willy," said Mr. Overs in a hearty voice after they had passed the time of day with other members of the congregation. "How about a little walk up to the Northern Star? Perhaps we'll even be able to pick out the window of the room where you'll be sitting, eh?"

Willy was stirred out of his morose silence. "No!" he said violently. "Not there!"

"Willy!" said his mother reproachfully, looking anxiously at his father, to see how he was taking this further display of insubordination.

But today Mr. Overs was trying to please.

"There's no need to go then. You'll soon be knowing the place well enough after all. We'll go around Ardwick Green and pick out the house where you'll be living when you're a great man, eh Willy?"

The procession moved off, Mr. Overs in his Sunday striped trousers and black coat, with Mrs. Overs in her plum-colored dress beside him, and Willy and George silent behind, fretting against the Sunday serge that scratched their legs and the collars that bit into their necks.

Downing Street, which on a weekday was noisy with trams and huge drays, was lapped in Sunday stillness. Walking at a Sunday pace the Overs approached Ardwick Green, and crossing over the road, passed behind the long strip of grass and sooty trees that was the Green, to the line of tall trim houses behind. It was where Dr. Parker had his brass plate, and on a normal day Mr. Overs would have pointed this out in a jovial way to the boys. But family conversation was frozen.

Ardwick Green was empty, except for one or two Sunday parties returning to roast mutton or roast beef like themselves. Shambling along behind his father Willy noticed nothing until he ran up against the buttons of Mr. Overs' coattails, and rousing himself out of his stupor found that the party had come to a standstill, and that the occasion of this sudden halt was a man with a heavy gray mustache, a top hat, and a length of gold watch chain adorned with seals stretched across his waistcoat. Beside him was a lady with a face like dough and eyes like currants.

"Mr. Ramsbottom," said Mr. Overs reverently. "Well, this is unexpected. But it's lucky, very lucky indeed, because I had it in my mind to speak to you about our young Willy here. Willy, this is Mr. Ramsbottom of the Northern Star. You've often heard me talk of Mr. Ramsbottom, haven't you, Willy?"

Willy, thrust forward, found himself staring into the watch chain.

"Hold your head up, Willy," said Mr. Overs in a loud jolly tone. "The Northern Star likes boys that looks people in the eye, isn't that so, Mr. Ramsbottom?"

To this Mr. Ramsbottom only cleared his throat, and said, "Ahem." With an effort Willy made his eye travel upward from the watch chain, over the black curve of Mr. Ramsbottom's waistcoat, up the high collar to the heavy mustache, and then he met Mr. Ramsbottom's eyes, bleak and cold, like a cod's.

"Our Willy wants to join the Northern Star, Mr. Ramsbottom, as I think I've told you before. So I said to Willy, I said, I'll talk to Mr. Ramsbottom about it next time he comes in for his cigars, and see if there's a place for you there. He's a likely lad, is our Willy, and keen on his studies and a hard worker and a steady boy. He'll do well, I'm sure of that. And he'll be thirteen and leaving school in the summer. As I've told him often enough, you can't start too early making your way up the ladder. Isn't that so, Mr. Ramsbottom?"

Mr. Ramsbottom cleared his throat once more,

settled his hands behind his back, and stared coldly with his cod's eyes at Willy. "I daresay if you bring the young man to see our Mr. Rapp he may be able to fix him up. He will have to content himself with running errands and little things of that sort at first, of course, and then if he can write a good, clear hand and is a careful, thorough worker, we might allow him to do a little copying."

"Well now, Willy, you heard what Mr. Ramsbottom had to say. What a chance for a lad to make good, eh? And when shall I bring him along, Mr. Ramsbottom? You can't be too early fixing up these matters as I'm sure you'll agree."

"You may bring the lad along whenever you please. And mention my name to Mr. Rapp, if you wish."

"Then with Easter coming up and school holidays I'll take the liberty of stepping along with him this week. I'm sure I'm very grateful for your kindness, Mr. Ramsbottom. I know Willy will do his best to be a credit to the Northern Star."

To this Mr. Ramsbottom made no reply, but raised his top hat a fraction from his head. Mrs. Ramsbottom gave them a final stare from her black, curranty eyes, and both parties moved on in the direction of the Sunday roast.

Mr. Overs had forgotten his Sunday pace and the difference there had been between him and

Willy. He was striding on with his eyes gleaming and his arms flailing. "There you are, Willy. Your first step on the ladder. You'll remember this day forever. When you come to set down your life like William Cobbett, you'll be able to tell them that the first step was took in Ardwick Green on a Sunday in March. On and on and up and up, Willy, and you'll fill that niche in the town hall!"

The gloomy depression that had lain over Willy during the past weeks was as nothing to the black misery that now engulfed him, dragging him down to the bottom of what felt like a dark pit from which it was impossible ever to escape. Though talk of the Northern Star and his life there had given him uneasy twinges from time to time in the past, he realized that he had never really believed that it would happen, any more than he believed that one day he would marry or leave home. But his father was talking about "this week"—and "this week" was not the unattainable future. You could measure it in hours. After that he would belong to that huge forbidding building, an ant trying to struggle up that long ladder to the top.

He stayed speechless all Sunday, and was awake much of the night, with George shifting noisily in his sleep. The clock in St. Luke's, Rutland Street, dolefully clanged the hours, bringing the Northern Star nearer to him. Heavy-eyed, with a dully aching head, he slouched to school in the morning, while George, who had given him up as a companion, ran on ahead to get a few minutes of football in the playground first.

He was standing listlessly by the door during the morning recreation, while the other boys jostled and whooped and screeched over the asphalted yard, kicking balls, thumping each other, running, and swarming up the iron railings, when Mr. Church came down the steps.

"Ah, William. I had been wanting to ask you, has your father decided upon what course your education should take?"

Willy gave a start, and looked at him numbly. He wished Mr. Church would go away. He didn't want to talk about his education when his father had already decided that it had got to stop.

"Father wants me to go into business," he said at last, hanging his head, and shuffling his feet.

"But have you discussed with him the possibility of going on to a grammar school?"

"He didn't like it."

"But have you informed your father that it is highly likely that you would be successful in winning a scholarship?"

"I did say that, yes."

"And what did he say?"

"He says he wants me to make my own way. Start in business young."

"But you would be handicapped without a good education. Does he know that?"

"Yes. I mean no. No, well, I dunno." Willy, near to tears of misery, wished desperately that the bell would ring and put an end to it all.

"I think the best plan would be if I called upon your father myself and talked the matter over with him."

Willy could only stare at the ground, appalled. That no good could come of this, was absolutely certain. But that did not worry him so much as the school world and the home world meeting, which they never had done before. The horror of it kept him from giving any attention to his lessons for the rest of the day. He just sat at his desk, holding his pencil, staring blankly in front of him, leaving his neighbor to turn the pages, and get out the right books. It was impossible to imagine what Audley Street would make of Mr. Church with his high, starchy collar, and his gold-rimmed glasses, and his way of talking like a book. But he did not have difficulty in imagining the high words that might pass between him and his father. He thought he would run away so that he wouldn't hear them, but when he got home his mother told him that his father wanted to see him.

Chewing his fingers in a fever of agitation he went through the parlor and peered through the curtains into the shop. Surely Mr. Church couldn't be there already? But Mr. Overs was talking politics, he could hear him—he must have somebody else. He pushed open the door and went in. It was Mr. Buller sitting on the other side of the counter, drawing on his pipe, and leaning on his stick. Mr. Overs swung around.

"Ah, Willy, there you are. I just wanted to tell you that I happened to see one of the clerks in Mr. Rapp's department, and I sent a message by him to say that I'd be bringing you in to see Mr. Rapp on Saturday morning. You get Mother to press your suit for you, and mind your shoes are shining like they never was before. If I was engaging a lad it'd be his shoes I'd look at—that, and whether he could look me in the eye. Wouldn't you be of that way of thinking, Mr. Buller?"

Mr. Buller pulled on his pipe and nodded.

"Ah, what couldn't you and me have done with opportunities like what are being put into young Willy's lap, eh, Mr. Buller? We'd have sprinted up that ladder pretty quick. But at young Willy's age I hadn't got a father or anybody to take an interest in me, I'd got to find what work I could, where I could, to bring bread back to those that needed it at home."

Mr. Overs was well launched, and might have gone on for a long time reminiscing in this vein, but at this point the shop bell jangled. The door opened more hesitantly than if there had been an Audley Street hand behind it, and in came Mr. Church, clasping his little attaché case. Heavily, Mr. Buller swiveled around to look at him. Willy did not give himself any time for looking, he fled into the parlor. But once there behind the door, he could not bring himself to leave; he knew he had to stay, to hear the whole horrible business.

"Mr. Overs, I presume?" said Mr. Church, clearing his throat.

"That's right."

"I am Mr. Church, William's teacher."

"That lad hasn't been up to no trouble, has he?" Mr. Overs' voice had a certain amount of anxiety in it.

"Oh, no, quite the contrary. William is a studious boy, and I wondered whether you had considered the possibility of his trying for a scholarship to a grammar school. He might even win a place to Manchester Grammar School. And from there, who knows, he might even go to a university. Just think of that, Mr. Overs, William at a university!"

Mr. Overs had listened to all this in silence. But it was an ominous silence. Willy, staring at his father's ramrod back through the glass just a cou-

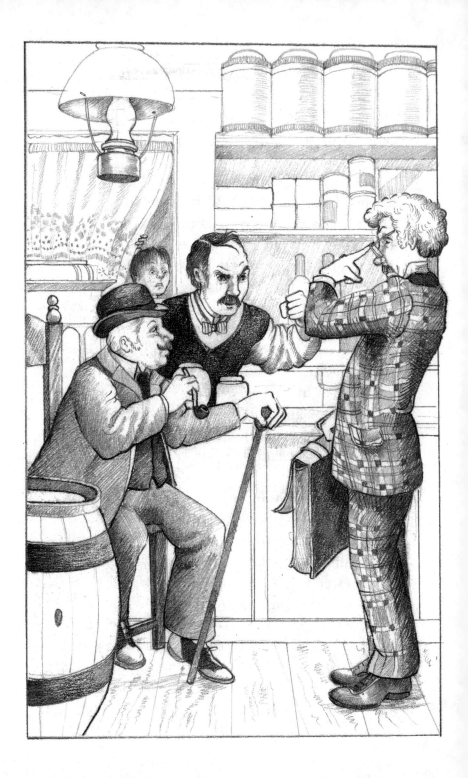

ple of feet from him felt despairing horror. Words
were going to come pouring out of his father now,
speechifying—he knew all the signs.

"And I say it's BUNKUM!" said Mr. Overs
loudly, and his fist descended on the counter with
a crash that made the jar of aniseed balls rattle.

"I assure you, Mr. Overs, that there is every like-
lihood of your son's getting a scholarship to such a
school, and this will cover all the fees."

Mr. Overs hit the counter another whack. "I'm
not worried about money, and I'm not worried
about Willy winning a scholarship, neither. Of
course he could. Win it standing on his head with
his feet waving in the air, and do it easy then. But
what I say is, no schools and no universities for
Willy. Schools and universities are for them that
can't pull themselves up another way. Willy's got
brains and sense. That'll get him where he wants.
Do you know what Cobbett says, Mr. Church?
Cobbett says, 'Education means *rearing up*, not
teaching to read and write.' And he said more, he
said, 'He is a learned man, who has great knowledge of others.' That's what I want for Willy, for
him to know about his own affairs, not to read
about what other people know. And you mark my
words, Willy'll be at the top of the tree when the
scholars are underneath groveling for the bits he

throws down to them. That's my view," said Mr. Overs, pulling out his handkerchief and loudly blowing his nose. "And Mr. Buller here will bear me out, won't you, Mr. Buller?"

"Ay," said Mr. Buller.

Mr. Overs cleared his throat of some of its emotion. "Rearing up," he repeated, "not reading and writing. We'll see who gets there first—our Willy, or the palefaced scholars creeping to their grammar schools. You look at those niches in the town hall, Mr. Church! Some of them may be empty now, but there's going to be another one filled before very long, and I know who's going to fill it. Eh, Mr. Buller? Haven't I said so all along?"

"Ay," said Mr. Buller again.

"So you see, Mr. Church, it's no good your coming here trying to win me over to your Latin and your Greek. Because my mind's made up, ever since I saw it set down in print by William Cobbett."

Mr. Church spoke at last. "I can only hope that you will never regret this decision. But I am afraid William will be very cast down. He loves his books."

"And that's just his trouble. He loves his books too well. A bit more of school and they'll have spoiled him for anything else. So he's leaving school when the summer's over and starting at the Northern Star. We've got a very good opening for him there, chance of a lifetime it is."

"I see," said Mr. Church bleakly. "Very well, I must take my leave." The shop bell jangled again, and he was gone.

· *12* ·

A Second Plunge

And so Willy ran away again. But this second time it was not adventure, but rage and shame that drove him out. He would never be able to hold up his head again, never be able to face school, after what his father had said to Mr. Church. He ran out into the hallway slamming the parlor door behind him so that the house rocked, and stormed down toward the back door.

"There's some pancakes here for you," called his mother faintly from the kitchen. "I'm keeping them hot."

"I'm not hungry," he shouted back, and burst out, down the steps, into the yard. But the yard was too small to hold him in the violence of his despair. Clenching and unclenching his hands he stood there, looking wildly around him. He wanted to do something destructive, something that would hurt. But the whitewashed walls of the yard held nothing except the garbage cans and the sheeted form of the tandem. On an impulse he strode over to this, tore its covers from it, and stood glaring at it. He wanted to kick down the house, kick down Audley Street and the Northern Star, and trample noisily on the ruins. Instead, he took the tandem, and the wheel of events that had taken charge of him when he was six, whirled him into the second great adventure of his life.

He did not really come to his senses until he had got to the top of the hill that led down into Stockport. He must have cycled five or six miles almost without noticing it in his mad fury. But by the time he could see the chimneys and the smoke of Stockport, and the huge viaduct that spanned the valley, the frenzied energy that had seized and swept him so far was leaving him, and he was, for the first time, aware of how heavy the machine was and how difficult to control. But now it was plunging down the hill and it was too late for common sense to reassert itself. As he lurched and jolted over the cobbles, clinging to the brown, felt handlegrips, he wondered if he had the strength to keep all that weight of iron on the road and himself on the seat. It was, in fact, the first rational thought he had had since he stormed out of the parlor.

He did reach the bottom safely, but only by narrowly missing a couple of trams and grazing a brewer's wagon, whose driver cursed him and flicked at him with his whip. Then he dismounted and stood by the curb, wiping his coat sleeve over his forehead, his knees shaking so much that he wanted to sit down. A lot of people gave him and his machine curious glances, but Willy hardly cared.

He was roused by a wailing howl that he ought to have known well enough, since he heard it day and night at home—the sound of a factory buzzer. Out of a yard down a side street came the clatter of hundreds of feet, and within a moment or two the workers had appeared: girls with their shawls drawn over their heads, and mobs of men. Shouting, laughing, and chattering, they swirled around Willy while he clutched defensively at the handlebars of his machine.

It attracted enough attention from the men. They clustered around, commenting on it, addressing remarks to each other and to Willy which he was too bewildered to hear.

"Well, aren't you going to give us an answer?" somebody bawled into his ear.

"What do you mean?" said Willy apprehensively.

"We wants a ride."

"No."

"You're a fine one. Got two seats and won't give
a ride."

"It isn't mine."

"Hear that? He's pinched it. Pinched a bike for
two. Did you ever hear the like! And won't let honest folk use it. Come on lads, get it from him." And
a thickset, red-faced youth laid his hands on the
back handlebars.

"No!" shouted Willy, scarlet with anger. "You
keep your hands off it, it's my father's."

"Let him alone," put in another voice, "he's only
a little lad. They don't mean no harm," it went on
reassuringly to Willy. "Don't you go crying."

"I'm not crying," said Willy furiously, though
tears of anger were standing in his eyes.

The crowd was melting away now, its interest
dwindling, and Willy was left with only two of the
mill hands. "They don't mean no harm," repeated
his protector. "They will have their bit of fun.
Where is your dad, then?"

"In Ardwick."

"Ardwick? Where do you come from then?"

Willy liked the look of him. He had fresh red

cheeks, and bright blue, merry eyes. "I came from Ardwick," he said, relaxing a little.

"What, rid from Ardwick all on your lonesome?"

Willy nodded.

"Well, you've got strength for such a spindleshanks. Are you going to take it all the way back then?"

"I suppose so," said Willy doubtfully. He had not started to think about his return.

"Why, you'll never get it there, a little lad like you, will he, Jack?" The youth turned to his companion, a lanky pale boy, with a long, solemn face. Jack shook his head gloomily.

"Nay, that he won't. Up this hill?" He sucked in his breath and pursed his lips. "Oh, no, that's not for little lads like him."

"You see what Jack says. You'll never get it there. Where do you live?"

"19 Audley Street," faltered Willy, beginning to feel miserably doubtful about those bright blue eyes which seemed to be having a secret joke with the other youth.

"And where's 19 Audley Street when it's at home?"

"It's my father's shop. Audley Street is near Grosvenor Street."

"Well, I'll tell you what we'll do, Jack and me, seeing as we're the kindly sort. We'll ride it back to Audley Street for you and hand it over to your dad. It'll get back safer that way, eh Jack?" He winked heavily at his companion. "Now Jack, you swing that leg of yours over the backseat and I'll take the front. And you stand away, young 'un, if you don't want to be rid down."

Dumbly, Willy stood back and watched the machine wobble across the road, down a side street, and disappear. Then he came to his senses. "Stop!" he screamed, and plunged across in pursuit, under the noses of a pair of tram horses. He dodged away from their feet, dimly hearing the driver shouting at him. There was no sign of the tandem down the side street. He went all the way down it, thrusting through the groups of shawled women and the children sprawled on the pavements, then made his way back to the main street. Perhaps it was all a joke, perhaps they would be bringing it back. He took up his post at the point where he had last seen them and scanned the road, turning his head anxiously to keep a watch in both directions.

But after a while he ceased to do even this, so hopeless did it seem. How could he ever face his father without it? How could he go back to Audley

Street? He was so frozen by the disaster that the cart driver who stopped by him had to shout several times before Willy noticed.

"I said, do you want a ride to the top of the town?" Willy still blinked in a dazed, uncomprehending way. "If you want a ride up the hill, get in," repeated the man. "What's up with you, lost your wits?"

Numbly, Willy allowed himself to be pulled up onto the shafts of the cart and sat down by the driver. He stared blankly over the jogging back of the horse, noticing nothing of what was said to him.

"Is this where you want to get down?" said the driver loudly. "My word, you seem a bit cracked up top."

Willy started and looked about him. They were out of the town now, but the road did not look familiar. "I don't know it here," he said feebly.

"I'll take you a bit farther then. I'm going to Sedgewick myself. That in your direction?"

Willy nodded. He had never heard of Sedgewick, but it was easier to agree.

"Where do you live then?" asked the carter after a quarter of an hour or so. "I said, where do you live?"

"In Ardwick," said Willy hastily. "We aren't

there yet, are we?" He peered around him. It was dusk now, but it did not look at all as though they were approaching Manchester. Indeed, it seemed that they were nowhere near a town. There was not a house in sight. Open fields stretched all around them and rose up to a crest of trees that stood black against the last white light of the departing day.

"Where's Ardwick then? You haven't said nowt about Ardwick all the blessed time you've sat here."

"In Manchester," Willy faltered.

"In Manchester? Why we've been going away from Manchester all the time. We was going away from Manchester when you got on. We must be eight miles from it now. You ain't fit to be at large. What are you going to do now?"

Willy shook his head dumbly.

"Well, I don't know neither. The best thing I can think of is to put you down at Staseley which we're coming to now. There's a carrier there who might be going into Stockport tonight—though I shouldn't think he would. Anyway, you'll not be wanting to go on this road no more. My word, I don't know what your folks are about, letting you out like this. Dressed quite respectable, too, otherwise I wouldn't have picked you up."

A few minutes later, around a corner of the road, the carter stopped, and stiffly Willy clambered down. "Ask for Mr. Starkey," called the carter. The horse clip-clopped into the twilight, and was gone, and Willy was left standing there.

It might have been the North Pole or the mountains of High Tartary for all he knew how to get home. He listened to the clop of hooves till silence overtook them, then, dazed, peered around him. Through the gathering darkness he could make out a church on a nearby slope and a cluster of small houses. He stood staring at them helplessly until his teeth began to chatter. "Ask for Mr. Starkey," the carter had said. He supposed he had better try.

He stumbled up a path through a garden he could not properly see, and found himself knocking on the door of what seemed to be a shop. Footsteps came after a bit, the door was unbolted, and slowly pulled open. He could not see who stood there but it was an old woman's voice who spoke.

"You've come at last, have you? I'd been expecting you for a long time, I had."

· *13* ·

WITH NANCE PRICE

Willy went in. It seemed to be expected of him. He stepped over the threshold and opened his mouth to explain.

"I'm looking for Mr. Starkey who's a carrier," he said hopelessly.

But the old woman allowed him to get no further. "Wait a bit, wait a bit, till I've bolted. You never know who's around these days. There now, come away in." And she shuffled off through what seemed to be a shop, though, in the darkness, Willy could make out little enough of what was in it. She pushed open a door, and stumbling after her, Willy found himself blinking in the light of a small, frowzy room. A rocking chair by the cinder-strewn fireplace seemed the only usable object in the room's clutter and confusion.

"It's just as you left it, Joey," said the old woman. "Except a bit older, maybe. None of us grows younger."

"My name's not Joey." Willy backed into the shop, alarmed. "I only came to ask for Mr. Starkey. I want to get home to Manchester."

The old woman came over to him, held him by the wrists, and peered at him shortsightedly. She was no taller than he was, and he found himself looking into filmy eyes and a face crisscrossed with lines. Her lips moved and she frowned as she scanned him. Then she dropped his wrists.

"No, you ain't Joey. Joey had brown eyes, dark as dark. 'Sides, Joey's been dead and buried these many years, I was forgetting. Who are you then? Are you somebody I know? My memory's that bad these days."

"You don't know me, I've never been here before. I just want to find Mr. Starkey because I want to get home to Manchester."

"Mr. Starkey? He's gone to Macclesfield tonight. He won't be back till tomorrow. But Manchester's a powerful way off, you must be tired. You sit down by my fire and warm up a bit. If you're not my Joey, there's a look of Joey about you."

Picking his way over the litter on the floor Willy sat down in the rocking chair and held his hands out to the fire. The warmth on his fingers made him realize how cold the rest of him was, and he shuddered.

"That's right, you look fair starved with cold. You wait a bit, I'll get you a bite to eat. I know what boys like."

She disappeared through a door behind him and Willy could hear her clattering dishes outside. All will and energy seemed to have left him. He sat back in the chair, and fell into a doze. Images of tandems, of Stockport street corners, and empty roads flickered feverishly through his mind, and he woke with a start, quite unable to remember where he was. The old woman was dragging a three-legged stool over the stone floor and setting a tray down on it.

"Here's your tea, Joey, just as you used to like it. I've made you a couple of potato cakes, you always was a one for them. And there's two eggs, boiled just as you always had them. You put the teapot on the hob yourself. There's a good boy, my back's that stiff these days."

It was difficult to eat, craning over the arm of the rocking chair. But Willy made a good meal. The disasters and the fears of the long day seemed to vanish into the darkness outside the cottage, and his mind was only on his tea, and the warmth

of the fire on his legs. The old woman poured him
out fresh tea as soon as he had emptied his cup,
and kept up a chatter which he really was too tired
to hear, and which he did not even pretend to
answer.

"You'll be wanting your bed now, Joey," she said
at last. "Your bedroom is just as it always used to
be. I'm not so good as I was at keeping the house;
my eyes aren't what they were. But your bedroom
is always ready for you. You just sit there till I fetch
a candle."

Willy was too drowsy to argue, and a few minutes later he was following her up a flight of stairs
which rose with ladderlike steepness from the corner of the room. At the top was a tiny room which
held a bed and a chest and enough space for one
person to stand. This was Joey's room, she told
him, and she would be going to her own bed now.
Willy was so tired that even throwing off his
clothes seemed something he would never be able
to achieve. He wondered wearily as he pulled off
his jacket whether he would have the strength to
bend down and unlace his boots. But at last he was
pushing his arms through Joey's nightshirt, which
he found under the bedspread, and falling grate-
fully into Joey's bed.

When he woke next morning he was completely

bewildered. He was staring at a ceiling whose patterns of yellow stains and cracks were utterly unfamiliar. He sat up in bed with fright and stared about him. It took him some minutes to piece it all together, and then as more and more of yesterday's events crowded into his mind, he felt so horrified at his predicament that he wanted to start out running to Manchester that minute.

He pulled on his clothes and went down the steep staircase. The old woman had heard him and was standing in the door at the far end of the room. "I've got your breakfast between two plates, Joey. Ham and eggs, seeing as it's a special day. It's been ready this hour or more. I didn't want to keep you waiting."

"I'm *not* Joey," he said loudly, "I'm William Overs from Manchester, and I've got to get home."

"Oh, ay, so you do be saying, I remember now. Well you eat this ham and eggs, there's no one else who will."

As he huddled on the edge of the rocking chair and gulped down the cold and leathery eggs he looked about him. The sun was coming through the small square window opposite and lighting the dirt and confusion of the little room. The panes of the window were filmed with grime and its tattered gingham curtain hung half off its rod. The gray ashes from weeks of fires strewed the hearth and had spilled over onto the greasy rag rug. And around the rug lay so much debris and rubbish, so many boxes and bits of old newspaper that it was a wonder that the old woman could ever make her way to the fireplace at all.

"I must go now." He stood up. The cinders and the crumbs under his feet felt gritty and he shifted them with distaste, remembering how his mother couldn't abide even a grain of sugar on the floor. "It sets my teeth on edge so's I could scream," she always said.

"Where are you going now?" The old woman clutched at his empty, greasy plate and peered at him with anxious suspicion.

"I've got to find Mr. Starkey and see if I can get back to Manchester."

She brightened a little. "If it's Mr. Starkey you're after he's in Macclesfield Tuesdays. Sometimes stays Wednesdays too. Oh, no, you won't be finding *him*." Cheered by this, she tottered off with the plate to the scullery.

"Where does he live?" called Willy desperately.

"Just over the way. But you won't be finding *him* today."

And it seemed she was right. At the cottage on

the other side of the road, the slatternly woman who opened the door told him the same story. Mr. Starkey always went out to Macclesfield on Monday night. He might be home by teatime today, that was, if he hadn't taken a drop too much with his friends, in which case it might be any time this side of Friday that he'd turn up.

Then Willy would have to walk back, setting off this minute; he couldn't hang around the place on the offchance that the carrier would turn up. Besides, even supposing he did happen to be going in the Manchester direction, how was Willy going to pay him—him without a penny piece in his pocket? He went back up the little garden path to tell the old woman—though garden you could hardly call it. It was a tangle of matted brown stalks through which the new green shoots of spring were beginning to thrust. He found her in the shop, dabbing fitfully at the floor with a broom.

"Seems the carrier won't be back till tonight," he said.

She nodded eagerly. "I knew it. Sometimes he don't come back till Thursday night, either. I hear him from my bed singing away."

"So I'd best be off now and try and walk it."

The eagerness faded from her face and she let

her broom fall. "You're not going now? Not when you've just come? Wait a bit and help me with the shop, things are getting that on top of me these days."

Willy looked at the disorder around him: the boxes piled aimless and tottering in front of the counter, the shelves scattered with dirty and rusting cans. Once they had been edged with colored paper, but most of this had torn away and hung down faded and trailing. No attempt had been made to dress the tiny shop window this century; it held a couple of advertisement placards which had fallen flat on their faces and sprawled on top of the dummy boxes of Bisto, from which the sun had drained all color. But all this could only be seen from the shop, so begrimed and cobwebby was the window. The old woman noticed his wandering eye.

"You see, it isn't what it was. I need a bit of help."

"But there's my father and mother, they'll be wondering about me," said Willy slowly. A wild idea was growing in his mind, and he was arguing it out with himself as much as with the old woman.

"Your father and mother?" she said puzzled. Then her mouth drooped. "Oh, yes, I was forgetting. You aren't Joey, you're somebody else."

"But I could write and say I was safe and then I could help you a bit."

Saturday was the day he was going to the Northern Star. If he could stay here until the end of the week, then he'd miss it, and everybody would be so angry that there wouldn't be any second chance.

"Yes, you do that. You tell them you're comfortable in Staseley with Nance Price and you're helping her out a bit. I need someone and that's a fact."

"Or maybe I ought to send a telegram, so as they can know more quickly?"

"Yes, yes, that's right. You tell them you're with Nance Price, that'll be enough."

And a few minutes later, clutching a shilling from the till which Nance Price had pressed into his hand, he was walking down the road toward the post office in Middleham to which he had been directed. He was nervous. He had to compose and send off a telegram, which nobody in his family, so far as he knew, had ever done before. But he was also in a state of mad high spirits, the like of which he had never known. It was almost as if he were drunk. He was in the country, by himself, he had escaped from the Northern Star, and nobody could find him. He ran, jumped, and whistled as he went along the narrow road with its pale green hedges and bright green fields beyond. Only a small doubt about the tandem nagged him sometimes; he oughtn't to have taken that only to lose it. But then, perhaps those men who had seized it, had returned it, as they said they would.

In the end he put a postscript about the tandem in the telegram. "Gone to country safe and well hope tandem comes back Willy." He had chewed the post office pencil to a rag by this time, but he was pleased with himself, and the tandem message so satisfied him that it was almost as if he had personally seen it returned.

His high spirits drooped a little when he got back to Nance Price. He had set his heart on turning the place right out, burning all the rubbish, rearranging the stock, and dressing the window. But he found that it could not be done—not at once anyway. The old woman hobbled anxiously around him, saying dolefully that she'd never be able to lay her hands on things if he moved them, and he had to spend so much time explaining what he had moved that he could make no headway at all.

They had some herring from the shop for dinner, and while she was out cooking them he got one shelf cleared, and had laid plans for dealing with the others.

"You sit by the fire this afternoon," he told her. "I'll look after the shop."

"There's not many that comes in these days. Still I don't know that . . ."

"I'll look after it," he said firmly. "My father keeps a shop so I know all about them." He stirred up the fire, turned the rocking chair so that it faced the warmth, and went into the shop, shutting the door.

There he worked feverishly, listening all the time for sounds that would indicate that Nance Price was hobbling in to stop him. He tore down the old shelf paper, he sorted through boxes, he investigated the contents of the shelves. He knew now how his mother felt about spring-cleaning—it was a sort of madness that seized you and wouldn't let you stop. So engrossed was he that the sound of the shop door being pushed open made him jump uncomfortably.

An old woman in rusty black stood there, the first customer he had seen all day. She was looking at him with deepest suspicion. "And who may you be when you're at home?"

"I'm helping Mrs. Price a bit," he said uneasily, and climbed down from the backless chair he had been using to reach the top shelf. "Can I get you anything?" He wiped his dusty hands furtively on the seat of his trousers.

"All in good time, all in good time, when I've had my think. Let me see now, what was it? Tea? Yes, it might have been tea, but I don't think it was, grate blacking more like. You fetch me down some grate blacking. So you're helping Nance Price are you? She didn't tell me nowt about it."

"I only came yesterday." He put a rusted tin of Zebo in front of her. "Here's the blacking."

"No, it wasn't blacking. It was matches. Them's what I want, matches. So you're helping Nance Price, well, well. Needs a bit of help, don't she. It'd been different if that boy of hers had lived."

"Joey?" ventured Willy.

"That's it, Joey. But Joey turned out wild. Not surprising, the way she gave in to him. I could have told her. But she didn't ask me, she was a proud 'un, she was. 'You're treating him far too soft,' I used to say to her, but she wouldn't listen. And then what does he go and do but get in trouble with the earl, and goes off to Australia and dies there. If you'd brought him up right he'd be here helping you now, I tell her. But she still don't listen. So now you've come to help her, have you? Well, you mind you don't get into trouble like what Joey Price did. Eh, eh—well, haven't you got a tongue in your head?"

"I don't know what Joey Price *did* do," said Willy, who was casting his eye furtively around the shop, impatient with longing to get on with his work.

"Poaching in the earl's woods, thieving, I don't

know what," said the old woman with deep satisfaction. "Made the place too hot to hold him. The earl did what he could. He came down his own self to warn Nance Price to keep the boy out of trouble, but she answered him proud as proud. She said things to him she never did ought to the gentry. And now look what it's done to her. Joey dead and gone, and her all alone in the world, and no one to turn to. I daresay the earl would have found a place for her in the almshouses up the road if it hadn't of been for all the proud way she carried on over that business about Joey. He takes good care of the folk here, does the earl. But not when they act uppish and haughty. What are you giving me matches for?"

"You said you wanted matches."

"Matches! What would I be wanting with matches? Me fire's alight. You give me some sugar, half a pound'll be enough, and mind your impudence. Yes, that's right, sugar, and you chalk it up on the slate and I'll pay Nance next time I sees her."

"I'll have to ask her first," said Willy.

"Ask?" screeched the old woman. "You'll be telling me I'm a liar next. Gives me matches when I asks for sugar, and then says he doubts me word. You give me those matches then and I'll give you your penny, but I tell you you're making a mistake when you tries to treat Mrs. Barnes like a common piece of dirt." And in a state of trembling indignation which made her head wag up and down, she hobbled out of the shop.

The noise of her departure brought Nance Price in. "That was Sairey Barnes in here," she said accusingly. "What was it she wanted?"

"She said she wanted blacking and sugar. But in the end she only took matches," said Willy, picking the penny off the counter and dropping it into the almost empty till.

"Sairey Barnes, she's a bit of no good. Cheat a blind man out of a crooked farthing, she would. And always poking her nose in where it isn't wanted and giving unasked-for advice. Sairey Barnes, I say, you go and sweep the dirt out of your own house and stop coming here and telling me what to do. I've been saying it for sixty years, and she still comes."

"She's gone now, though," said Willy. He was fidgeting to get back to his work of putting the place to rights. Nearly the whole afternoon had gone by and he had so little to show for it. "Shall I go and stir up the fire for you so's you can sit by it again?"

"I've had enough of sitting for a bit. I'll look to

the shop. When Sairey Barnes is about you need to keep your eyes skinned, you do."

"But I can watch her," insisted Willy. "Anyway, she's gone now."

"Ay, but she'll be back, and up to no good, I know her tricks. No, you're a good lad, you go out and play a bit. Lads like play, I know my Joey did. Here, I tell you what, you take this story. It's the sort of story lads like, lads like my Joey. You put it in your pocket. There you are. Now you be off, but don't get into any mischief, mind, and keep out of them woods of the Earl's or you'll be in trouble."

And so Willy found himself wandering down a tangled garden out somewhere in the country, he did not for the life of him know where, on a bright April afternoon when he should by rights have been bending over his books in Ardwick. Wherever it was, it was a far prettier place than Ardwick, though it was not this that he noticed at first, but the stillness of it all. There was nobody in the road, the handful of cottages might have been uninhabited for all that he could see, and beyond them stretched broad grassy spaces, empty of life too.

He hesitated, and then walked up in the direction of the church that stood rosy pink in the sun, on a hill above the road. It looked so soft and pale; he had never seen a church before that wasn't coal black. A little beyond it was a school, with an empty playground next to it. Such a small school it seemed after the gaunt three storeys of his own. There was a window open, and childish voices inside were singing a hymn. Beyond the school and its playground came a range of little houses, all joined together, bordered by one trim garden. The row of neat little front doors, each with a single window beside it filled for the most part with plants, intrigued him, and he loitered and stared. They had something of the look of the village school about them, and yet they were houses, each with its own pretty chimney, twisted like a barley sugar stick. It was as his eye wandered down from the chimneys to the gables that he got the answer, in a carved stone tablet in the middle: "The Lady Alice Almshouses. Erected 1863 to the memory of a beloved daughter by the Earl and Countess de Staseley." These then must be the almshouses where old Mrs. Price might have been living, if, according to old Mrs. Barnes, she hadn't answered the earl "proud as proud." He liked the look of them; they were cozy and snug and he wouldn't mind spending the rest of his life in one.

He went ambling on, with no particular purpose in his walking. The village was now left behind, and he was walking under trees that arched over the road and splashed pale spring sunshine in bright patches through their bare branches. This was proper country, this was. All his life, ever since he had seen those vistas of grass and flowers and trees in Whitworth Park, he had thought of what it must be like to walk in proper country where there were hundreds of trees, where you could wander without rough boys mocking at you and angry men chasing you away, and where the ground was soft, and not hard and paved. Over the hedge there the ground looked soft enough. He looked for a gate, saw none, then straddled the ditch and pushed his way through a gap on the other side.

His feet sank in dead leaves which came up to his ankles, and every now and then he trod on a twig that cracked like a pistol shot. He walked on through the trees, half tipsy with elation. This really was adventure, walking into the unknown, waiting to discover what lay beyond the trees. Light shining beyond the smooth green and gray trunks warned him that the woods were coming to an end. Half of him wanted them to go on forever so that he could continue in this excitement, but the other half hurried him on to see what was beyond.

It was a marvelous sight. There at the bottom of a rough grassy slope lay a huge sheet of water, shining white in the sun. Over on the other side

were more woods, dark outlines massed against the sky, here and there splashed with bright green where one of the trees was coming into leaf. And in front of them, just beyond the water, looking like some beautiful toy, was a house.

It would have been huge if you were near it, of course. But from where Willy stood it looked as if it had been put there by a child—neat, square, white, with scores of windows flashing and glinting in the sun like diamonds. Willy stared at it, marveling. Then he sat down to look at it better. There was a chilly wind in spite of the sun, so he hugged his knees as he leaned his chin on them. Out on the water below, the dark shape of ducks bobbed, and he could hear ducks, or something like them, rustling unseen among the rushes at the edge, and calling with a harsh, lonely cry.

As he watched, one of the ducks flapped its wings and rose out of the water, running along the surface, it seemed, with silver drops falling from its feet. He was so excited he ran down to the water shouting.

It was then that he heard shouts from behind him. Out of the woods, seemingly very angry, lumbered a heavy man in brown velveteens.

· 14 ·

FACE-TO-FACE WITH
THE ARISTOCRAT

He was very angry indeed, there was no doubt about that, and it was Willy that he was heading for. Not knowing what it was all about, Willy stood there gaping, and a few seconds later the man's red, gray-whiskered face was thrust into his, and he was being shaken violently.

"I've cotched you red-handed, you young imp. This time you're not getting away, you're coming with me to his lordship!"

Willy was being joggled so uncomfortably that he couldn't speak, but he suddenly felt six years old again and at the mercy of the Whitworth park keeper. It was the same thing all over again. He had thought then that the parks belonged to everybody, and he had been wrong. At twelve years old he had thought that country and woods belonged to no one, and there it seemed he had been wrong too.

"You were here on Sunday, weren't you, and you got away then, but you're not getting away now. Oh, no you're not." And with a large, cold hand down Willy's collar he gave him another shaking that nearly throttled him.

"I wasn't here on Sunday," shouted Willy, struggling to get free. "I never was here before in my life. I don't know where it is or who it belongs to."

"A likely story. And what's that in your pocket? Snares I daresay."

Guiltily, Willy crammed his hand into his pocket and felt a book and then remembered how Mrs. Price had thrust it there. The whiskered velveteens saw the movement and pounced.

"*Flash Jim the Cracksman,*" he read out. "So that's the sort you are. Thieving, not poaching this time, is it?"

He was now dragging Willy at a furious rate over the rough grass with Willy too dazed and bewildered to resist. Or to pick up his feet properly either, for after a few yards a tussock tripped him up and sent him sprawling full face on the ground with his captor, taken off his guard, on top of him. The fall, and the weight of the man, completely winded Willy, and he lay there gasping; he was hardly aware of the faint calls from the distance, and was startled when the man shouted back.

"Here is his lordship," he said with grim satisfaction, getting to his feet. "And he'll have seen for himself the sort you are, tripping people up and all—quite the smart young criminal, eh? Well, you'll find that don't wash this time! Get up, can't you, didn't nobody ever tell you how to behave to the gentry?"

And so, muddy, dazed, with a swimming head, Willy Overs faced the aristocracy for the first time. All his life he had been hearing about them from his father. With flailing arms and a voice thick with emotion Mr. Overs had denounced them and had told his sons about the long and bitter struggle of the common man to wrest his rights from the aristocratic overlords who sought to trample him into the dirt. It could not be said that Willy had given them very much thought on his own account, but when he did, he vaguely pictured them as dressed-up dandies strutting around, waving aside with be-ringed hands the pleas of starving beggars. Or alternatively, as the cruel tyrants that Dickens had described in *A Tale of Two Cities*, using abject peasants as driven beasts.

But what he saw fit neither of these pictures. Coming down the slope in a baggy tweed knickerbocker suit, was a man who was remarkably like his father. He was lean, he had a ginger mustache, and he strode along with the same sort of energy. His voice was not the same, though, it was more like Mr. Church's at school, rather high-pitched and clipped.

"Bastable, Bastable," he was calling, "who have you got there?"

"It's one of those little devils, begging your lordship's pardon, who've been laying snares up in the woods and stoning the ducks. Caught him in the act, I did. And look what I found on him!" He brandished *Flash Jim the Cracksman*.

"I *wasn't* setting snares," shouted Willy, "nor stoning the ducks. I've never been here before in my life."

"That's no way to speak to his lordship," said the man in velveteens, scandalized. "You mind your manners now. And if you weren't up to some mischief what were you up to, I'd like to know?"

"I was just looking at the water," said Willy defiantly.

"A likely story," sneered the velveteens, "and I suppose you was just looking at the water on Sunday morning and loosing a few stones on the ducks accidental like?"

But before Willy had time to protest again, his lordship broke in. "Sunday morning, Bastable, Sunday morning? You were surely in church?"

This, rattled out at top speed in a high voice, seemed to cause the man in velveteens considerable embarrassment, and certainly diverted his attention from Willy. His reply was not wholly audible, but he said something about looking after his lordship's interests.

"Interests, interests? My interests are the welfare of my tenants and employees, yes, their welfare, Bastable."

Bastable was thoroughly discomfited, Willy could see that. There was a pause, and then he tried to renew the attack. "Well, what are we going to do with him, m'lord? Turn him over to the police, or shall I give him a good birching? Let 'em learn through their skin, that's what I say."

"*I* will talk to the boy, Bastable. And the first thing I shall want to know is why he is not in school?"

It was now Willy's turn to be thrown into confusion. He was prepared to refute heatedly all the accusations of having been there on Sunday and having ill-used the ducks. But he could not deny that he was playing truant from school. Bastable was triumphant.

"You've cotched him there, m'lord. And look at what he was reading too."

Gingerly his lordship took the gaudy red and

blue book. "Thank you, Bastable. There is no need for you to wait."

With a last malignant look at Willy, the man in velveteens stumped off, and Willy, ill at ease, ransacking his mind for excuses, waited for the wrath that was to come.

It did not come at once. First his lordship fumbled in his breast pocket for some seconds before he pulled forth an eyeglass attached to a long gold chain, which he screwed into one eye. Then lowering a ginger eyebrow over it and holding out the book at arm's length, he scrutinized the cover. Willy looked at it, too, for he had not examined it before. There was a picture of a burly tough with a mask over his face, kneeling beside a heap of jewels. His lordship gave it long consideration. Then he picked open the yellowed pages and drew in his cheeks as if in pain.

"Do you know what I would have done if I had found one of my own sons reading this gallows literature? I would have made him wash out his eyes with soap, yes soap, to cleanse him of the filth contained within it! Do you know what gallows literature is, boy?"

Dazed by the completely unexpected turn that things had taken, Willy shook his head.

"It is reading matter like this that drives boys

into crime, men to the gallows! It is poison, the rankest poison. Better that you had never learned to read than that you polluted yourself with this." His eyeglass fell out, and he sawed the air with the gaudy book. "And your mother, boy, have you a mother? Would you show this to your mother? Would you show it to your sister? I would grieve if any of my boys at Staseley School corrupted themselves with this vile trash. What is your school, boy?"

"Rutland Street Elementary," stammered Willy, caught off his guard.

"Then why are you not *in it?*"

"Well, I thought I'd—I'd help old Mrs. Price a bit," said Willy, casting his mind around wildly for excuses.

"And does your schoolmaster know of your absence? Where is Rutland Street, in Stockport?"

Willy quailed before that bright blue stare. He wasn't prepared for questions of this sort. "It's in Manchester," he muttered.

"And why are *you* not in Manchester?"

Now Willy was completely floored. Licking his lips, he looked at those bright eyes, that ginger mustache, so disconcertingly like his father's, and not a word could he produce. Panic surged over him, and he ran away.

As he pounded up the hill and floundered

through the leaves in the wood, listening wildly for pursuing footsteps, he felt more humiliated than he had ever felt in his life. He had made a right fool of himself all around, wandering into that lord's woods, getting lectured as though he was a common thief, and then letting his legs carry him away like that instead of sticking it out.

No one chased after him; the only sound in the woods was the swishing of the leaves and the snapping of twigs as he ran on. He burst through the hedge, jumped into the road, and wiped a coat sleeve over his scarlet, sweating face. Then at a jog trot, he went back to the village.

The flavor had gone out of the work in the shop; he was nervous of pursuers, for one thing, and all the time he was cleaning up the shelf that held the candy jars, he kept looking over his shoulder, half expecting the velveteen breeches of Bastable, or the tweed knickerbockers of the lord to appear through the shop door. How much had he told the lord? Not his name, certainly, but he had said where his school was, and he thought he might have mentioned Nance Price's name, though he couldn't be sure. Was what he had done bad enough for them to come ferreting him out?

He tried asking Nance Price. "Those woods up the road?" he said casually. "Do they belong to anyone?"

Old Mrs. Price was sitting on the backless kitchen chair, looking in front of her. "Them woods, Joey? You keep out of them woods. You'll get took up if you go there."

"Who do they belong to?" said Willy loudly.

She looked at him blankly. "They're the earl's woods, of course."

"Is he angry with people who go into them?"

"Nobody's allowed in there," she said with finality.

"Is it against the law even when you're doing no harm?" he insisted. "Even when you're only looking?"

"The earl won't have nobody there," she repeated.

"But what does he do if they do go?"

"He doesn't let anybody go."

"But if you do go and you do get caught, what does he do?" Willy felt as though he was grappling with a Manchester fog, trying to get a straight answer from old Mrs. Price. He searched for some way of breaking through. "What did he do to Joey?"

The question penetrated the fog, and produced tremendous agitation. "You leave my Joey alone. They're always on at me about him. He's a good boy if they only leave him alone. It was all that Sairey Barnes's doing, I know that, she went and told the keepers—said she found pheasant's feathers in my garden. And what was she doing poking around my garden, I'd like to know? Then the earl came and told me wicked falsehoods about Joey and his doings. It's no good telling me all that, I said. It's what Mrs. Barnes and that lot has been telling me and I don't believe a word of it. My Joey's a good lad but he don't like being preached at and interfered with. I know he don't work regular, I said, but lads don't like work, and I can keep him. Then the earl said he'd give Joey twenty pounds to emigrate to Australia and have a new start in life. He'll never take it, I said. He's too fond of his home. But he took it and he went, and I never saw him again." Nance Price's voice dropped mournfully. Then it rose sharply. "And all through that Sairey Barnes poking her nose in."

All this was precious little comfort to Willy. It looked as though the earl was a vigilant man, and old Mrs. Barnes a mischief-maker, and that he was unlikely to escape the consequences of being found in those woods, however innocent his intentions had been. He spent an uneasy evening, starting at every sound, and a restless night, with anxiety about his pursuers mingled with pricking doubts about home, coming between him and sleep.

What sleep he did succeed in capturing was interrupted in the very early morning by a hubbub of bird noises. Wearily he blinked at the pale gray square of uncurtained window. Never had he heard such an uproar, such a shrilling and whistling and calling, as if every bird in Christendom was screaming defiance. It was worse than the buzzer at home, and quite impossible to sleep through. As he lay there resentfully, wondering whether they would ever tire of it and stop, the thoughts which had kept him awake earlier started whirling around his head again, the nagging worry of whether the earl and the keeper would find him here, the worry about what they might be thinking at home and what had become of the tandem. It was like a wheel circling; first one was at the top of his mind, then the other.

But then, quite suddenly, a new and startling thought joined them. He didn't know how it came there, it was through no conscious effort on his part, but once it arrived it became so powerful that it drove everything else out. Supposing his father bought Nance Price's shop! She couldn't want to keep it on, and his father would make a real success of it, he knew that. The idea took shape in his mind; he began working out the new lines they would stock, how they would dress the window, rearrange the shelves. Then he moved on to the house itself, where they would put the piano, and how he would dig the garden, and how it might put an end to first Sundays.

He fell asleep with a confused idea of Uncle Harold coming around in the trap to try to sell them stuff, and woke when the sun was streaming in through the window. Nance Price was up, he could hear her downstairs fumbling with the fire and raking out the cinders. When he had pulled his clothes on he ran down to her with his plans throbbing in his head.

"Would you sell this shop?" he asked breathlessly.

It was difficult for her clouded mind to take in this idea, especially presented so suddenly, and he had to repeat it slowly several times over. "There's none would want to buy a place like this," she said doubtfully. "There's not much trade these days."

"But would you sell it?"

"I don't know about that. Where would I live? A body's got to lay her head somewheres."

"But if you had somewhere to live—the alms-houses or somewhere?" persisted Willy.

"Maybe. But I don't like change and that's a fact. Now if you were to stay along with me, Joey, and not go traipsing off again, we'd get along very nicely."

It was useless pushing the matter any further,

but all morning Willy's mind worked on it. From time to time he would stop in his slow work of cleaning the shelves, straighten himself, and holding a sticky bottle of sauce in one hand and a rag of a duster in another, stare fixedly and unseeingly into the dark spaces of the shop, considering some new aspect of the Overs' proprietorship of the shop. He was just wondering whether his father would agree to putting "Overs and Son" on the sign when he saw the earl.

To be sure, the earl could not see him; he was riding down the road beyond the little garden, and his face was not turned toward the shop at all. But it gave Willy such a fright that the sauce bottle slithered through his fingers and crashed to the floor. He did not stop to pick it up, but scooped up a mound of rubbish from the floor and fled, through the parlor, into the murky little scullery beyond, where Nance Price was at this moment.

"I'm just going to make a fire in the yard to burn all this," he shouted at her, and, without waiting to see whether she understood, he had tugged open the back door and slammed it behind him.

The yard was a forsaken wilderness of thorny bushes which tore at his clothes as he tried to force a way through. It was bounded by a low moss-grown wall. This was what he had his eyes on. He flung down his armful of boxes and papers and scrambled over.

And there he lurked with a pounding heart for hours—or so it seemed, straining his ears for sounds of pursuers, crouching with cramped legs, pricked by the dead stalks of nettles. But he couldn't hear anything except the chirrup of birds; no voices, no footsteps, nothing.

When he straightened himself at last, his legs were so stiff that he nearly fell over. Awkwardly he pulled himself over the wall, stood listening for a moment, and then furtively pushed open the back door a crack. The cottage was lapped in silence. He snatched up a box of matches, and withdrew.

By dint of feeding the flames with dead wood and weeds in the yard, he managed to keep his bonfire going all the rest of the morning. He did not leave it, in fact, until Nance Price pulled open the scullery door. He was half-poised to fling himself over the wall again, and looked at her apprehensively.

"Oh, now I see you. I'd been wondering where you was. Your dinner's waiting."

He came over slowly. "What time is it, then?"

"Dinnertime, I reckon, the children have gone past out of school, I heard them. There's some pickled onions and cheese in the parlor."

The smell of onions and vinegar mingled with the fumes of bonfire smoke from his clothes as he sat on the stool in front of the fire, gnawing at the stale bread that had been laid out for him. Nance Price was shuffling around the room, muttering to herself and fumbling in the debris that was strewn upon every surface. Somehow Willy had to find out whether there had been anybody looking for him.

"Did you have a busy morning?" he ventured at last.

The mouselike scrabblings and rustlings stopped, and Nance Price came over and peered at him.

"What was that you said?"

"I wondered whether you had had a busy morning."

"Busy? No, it wasn't what you'd call busy, there isn't much trade these days. They're on at me about Joey, though—they can't leave the boy alone."

Willy's hunk of bread fell onto the cracked plate. He felt very cold. "Who's on at you about Joey?"

"They all are. They ask questions. I don't know where he is, I said. And if I did I wouldn't tell you. He's a good lad and he's settled down and he's helping his old mother. But they've gone away now, and I daresay they won't trouble me anymore. It was that Sairey Barnes's doing, and that's a fact. If ever there's trouble it's Sairey who's brewed it. It was like that when we was girls at school and it's like that now. I saw her going tittle-tattling around the place this morning, stirring up mischief."

"But what was she saying?" asked Willy. His tongue felt too big for his mouth.

"I don't know what she were saying, but it were mischief, you can stake your soul on that. Now if you've ate your dinner, you look to the shop for an hour or two, there's a good lad. Just so that I can have a bit of a sit down, I'm fair wore out and that's the truth."

There was no doubt about it, Willy had to go. He took a pail of water with him, reckoning he could crouch down and scrub the floor behind the counter, so that nobody would be able to see him through the shop window. He remembered, too, with some compunction, the wreckage of the sauce bottle on the floor.

But nobody came while he was scrubbing, and nobody came while he was finishing his work on the shelves. Nance Price was dozing in the rocking chair by the fire and never stirred when he went through to the scullery to fetch more water. The afternoon wore on, and a hubbub of shouts from up the road showed that the children were coming out of school. They streamed past, cuffing and pulling off each other's caps, kicking stones, and dragging their boots over the road surface. Willy stood at the back of the shop watching them through the window. He felt lonely suddenly. That was where he ought to be, coming home from school, and he stared out almost longingly, hoping that someone would turn and come up the path to spend a ha'penny in the shop. But it was clear that the schoolchildren had long ago abandoned any idea of their being able to find something to buy in Nance Price's shop. They did not give the shop a glance, but jostled past in a cheerful, noisy mob.

Willy wriggled his shoulders and shook his head and picked up the scrubbing brush again. There was no use in standing mooning like this, he had better get to work before Nance Price came out, and he might as well make a start on the window.

He was leaning forward, trying to wipe down some of the cobwebs that draped the corners of the meager little hollow that answered for a shop window when he heard the clop of hooves. Perhaps it was the earl coming back! The hooves came nearer and stopped just out of sight. There were voices in the road, then footsteps. The gate was pushed open, and down the path came Mr. Overs.

· 15 ·

AUDLEY STREET AGAIN

Willy was so startled that he fell forward into the limp cardboard boxes that strewed the window, and lay there, staring out. His father looked grimly resolute, his red whiskers ferocious. The old, childish fear of The Stick smote Willy; he lay there, powerless, gaping at the striding figure.

The door was flung open with a force that made it hit the wall and bounce back; the bell jangled wildly. Willy pulled himself out of the window and stood there abjectly. He was still holding the duster; to put it down now would seem that he wasn't taking the arrival of his father seriously, so he clutched it awkwardly in a hand that he thrust behind his back. His father was breathing heavily.

"And just what do you think you're a doing of?"

Willy licked his dry lips. "I was helping them here," he faltered.

"Helping them here," repeated his father heavily. "And not giving a Chinese fig for what was going on at home."

"But I did send a telegram, honest I did," broke in Willy. "I sent it yesterday. And some chaps in Stockport took the tandem, before I realized what they were doing. Then somebody gave me a lift in his cart, I thought he was bringing me back to Manchester, but I fetched up here instead. Did they bring the tandem home? They said they would."

"The *tandem*!" said his father in disgust. "Yes, they brought that back right enough. Left it outside the shop. That Mrs. Jericho saw them do it and was kind enough to come in and tell us. But what about us? You talking about the tandem when all the time we was all off our heads with worry, and all the street talking, and the police out looking, and your mother screaming about the canal all night."

"But didn't you get my telegram?" repeated Willy miserably. All that his father had said had come as a completely new idea. He had never imagined them carrying on at home like this—his parents had always seemed so calm and steady. He clung now to the telegram as the only way he had of putting things right.

"Oh, we got your telegram, but that was the morning after I thought we'd have to put your mother in a mad house, she was in that state. And what did the telegram tell us? Only that you weren't dead. And what do you say now? Not that you're sorry, oh, no. You just ask me about the tandem."

"But . . . but I thought you liked it."

"Like it!" His father drew in his breath as if for an eruption of fury. "I'd like to throw it in the canal. You wouldn't have got so far if it hadn't been for the tandem. Well, are you coming now?"

"I suppose so," muttered Willy.

"You *suppose* so!" shouted his father. "Willy Overs, I can't believe you're my child. I've come all this way, hired a cart from Stockport to carry me here, and now you say you suppose you'll deign to come with me."

Slippers shuffled over the stone floor of the parlor, and Nance Price appeared in the doorway. "Is it the poaching they've come about, Joey boy? Oh, I did tell you there'd be trouble! Why didn't you heed when I told you!"

"It's Mrs. Price," Willy whispered urgently to his father. "She owns the shop. Sometimes she thinks I'm her son. I've got to go home with my father now," he said loudly. "I'm needed at home."

"He's got no business to be here at all," said Mr.

Overs angrily. "You should have sent him packing when he first came."

Mrs. Price looked from one to the other uncomprehendingly. "Got to go now, Joey? And you barely come. You always was one for wandering, though. It's the fault of them interfering nosey parkers, I'll warrant. They was around again this morning asking questions."

Willy forgot everything else in his pity for this forlorn old woman. "I've tried to tidy things a bit." It was the only crumb of comfort he could offer.

Her eyes wandered to the shelves. "It don't seem like it used to be," she said helplessly.

"It's just a bit tidier. You'll soon find your way around. I have to go now, but thank you very much for letting me stay." Then he remembered the duster, and put it down by the rusty scales on the counter. "Good-bye," he said awkwardly. There was nothing much more he could say with his father standing there grimly.

In silence, father and son tramped out over the quarry-tiled floor, now patchily clean where he had scrubbed, with flecks of suds here and there. From the gate onto the road he looked back. Nance Price was standing, shading her eyes with a shaking hand.

"Good-bye," he called. "Thank you for what you did."

Faintly, as he climbed up into the trap, he heard her voice. "Why do you have to be wandering off all the time, Joey? And Australia now. I'll never see you alive again, Joey."

The trap jogged up the road past the church, the school, and the almshouses—the way he had walked the day before. Nobody said anything. The driver, having given Willy a curious glance, withdrew his attention, sunk his chin into the dirty white muffler that looked as though it hadn't been off him since the beginning of the winter, and flicked at his horse from time to time with the reins. Willy did not look at his father. He stared at the hunched shoulders and the greasy overcoat of the driver until his eyes burned, and thought about Nance Price, bewildered and forlorn, left by herself once again.

Someone was calling. He looked down, and there was old Mrs. Barnes, standing by the side of the road. She was smiling malevolently, or so it seemed to him, and wagging her head. "So they came and fetched you out, did they?" Her glance flickered over Mr. Overs. "I thought they would."

The trap was trundling along now under the bare, black trees of the woods where Willy had wandered yesterday, blissfully imagining that woods, like the sky, belonged to no one in particular. The same woods where Joey Price had gone trespassing all those years ago. And there was Joey's mother still waiting, with his bed all ready for him.

"Father," he said hesitatingly.

"Yes?"

"Mrs. Price—she's the one you saw who thinks I'm her dead son—she would sell that shop."

"What's that to me?"

"It's just . . ." Willy faltered, staring at the gritty white rim of the trap wheel as it lurched and wobbled on its way around, "just that I thought you might like to buy it, and we could get it all straight and run it properly and I could help you. I'd like to do it, really. I enjoyed no end working to straighten things up and . . ."

Willy never finished what he was going to say, for his father broke in. "You enjoyed yourself no end, did you? And all the time we was hunting for you, and the police was looking through the mortuary to see if there was your corpse picked out of the canal, you was enjoying yourself. And I tell you all this, and how your mother's near out of her mind, and instead of being sorry all you can do is ask if I'll buy you a shop to play with!"

Willy, appalled, with tears welling up in his eyes, looked from his father to the back of the man who was driving them. The shoulder blades that stuck out through the overcoat were rigid, unmoving; the head in its greasy hat remained sunk forward, in spite of all this torrent of anger being poured out behind him.

"I didn't mean . . ." whispered Willy. Then he stopped, because he didn't know what it was he didn't mean, and he couldn't bear to say any more with a listener there.

"Oh, yes, you meant it all right," said his father loudly. "It's all part and parcel of your behavior all the time — never thinking of anybody except Willy Overs."

In spite of the shame of being overheard, Willy was lashed by the hateful injustice of this. "I wasn't thinking of myself," he said, hot with rage. "It was because of Mrs. Price."

"So what you're trying to say is that someone you've known for two days means more to you than your own father and mother? That's what it is, eh?"

Angry, baffled, almost defeated, Willy groped for a retort. But his brain didn't feel equal to any proper arguing. It was all so unfair, so unjust, to expect him to explain things with a complete stranger sitting a few inches away. He glared hotly at the greasy hat, longing to ram it down over the wearer's ears and extinguish him. Then, over the man's shoulder he saw a horse with a rider on it turn out of a concealed gateway into the road. It was the earl.

"Stop!" shouted Willy, prodding between the shoulder blades in front of him. "I want to get down!" He was already standing up in the swaying trap and hoisting himself over the side. He landed on all fours in the dust, the wheel narrowly missed one of his hands, and his father was shouting at him. But he picked himself up and ran forward. The horse ahead of him was startled at this apparition running at it full tilt, and shied sideways.

"Steady, steady, you stupid lad," said the high–pitched voice that Willy remembered so well and with such a sense of humiliation. "What do you think you are about?"

"It's about Nance Price," gasped Willy breathlessly, looking over his shoulder, fearful in case his father and the trap would carry him off before he got the words out. "You need to do something about her. You carried on about people's welfare. Well, you do something about hers. She's too old to be looking after that shop; she's all muddled in her wits. You put her in that almshouse with your name on it!" There was plenty more he wanted to say, but he had run out of words and out of breath, and stood there gasping and heaving.

The earl, with pursed lips, was fumbling in a pocket. Then he produced his eyeglass and put it on and frowned down at Willy. "Why, you are the boy there has been all this to-do about. You have already caused a great deal of disturbance. You seem to be a very naughty boy."

It deflated Willy completely, to be called a naughty boy as though he were five years old. "I want you to do something about Nance Price," he repeated, but his voice was trembling, and he knew he would cry if he stayed any longer. He ran back to the trap which had stopped only a few yards off, and without looking at the faces of the two men in it, not wanting to see what they had made of all this, he hauled himself up, mounting on the hub of the wheel and rocking the trap perilously.

"Well," said the driver without turning around. "You finished your little larks for a bit?"

"I just want to go home," said Willy thickly.

But the trap still had to pass the earl on his horse. The driver's head moved to stare at him as he came riding past. Willy lowered his own and glowered at the dirty floorboards so that he would not see the earl's face.

"Who is the father of this boy?" he heard the earl say.

"I happen to be his father." Willy could tell by his father's breathing that he was preparing for battle. But the earl was too quick for him.

"Well, see that he stays in school, my good man. Education is now within the grasp of every child in this land and it behoves parents to see that their children avail themselves of it. And you, young man, keep away from evil books in future. Education was provided to uplift the mind, not to corrupt it!" And with a clattering of hooves and a jingling of the bit, the horse and its rider moved on.

It had diverted Mr. Overs' attention from Willy for the moment. "And just who does he think he is?" Now it was his turn to rise in his seat. Swaying, he stood brandishing his arms at the retreating rider. " 'My good man' he says! You put me down, and I'll go and ask him what he means by 'my good man!' Who is he, anyway? What's been going on between you and him, Willy, I'd like to know?"

He was obviously at the point of saying a great deal more, but the driver broke in. "Best sit down, mate. We'll have to get moving; all this stop and start, stop and start, it's going to cost you a fair packet by the time we get to Stockport."

Whether any more was, in fact, said, Willy was

not in a state to notice. He sat in a seething whirl-
pool of his own thoughts, and was not even aware
that they had arrived at Stockport until his father
angrily tugged at his arm to get him out of the
trap. He toiled up the long flight of steps to the
platform, got limply onto the train when it came,
and sat rigidly squeezed up in a corner, looking
out at the back gardens and the rooftops that
raced along below.

Perhaps it was something about one of the dere-
lict gardens that ran right down to the railway, or
perhaps it was a tumbledown roof below that suddenly reminded him of Miss Chaffey, who had
faded from his mind as though she had been one
of the nightmares of his winter illness. Miss
Chaffey—she was the only one with any money
that he knew, maybe she could be persuaded to
help out Nance Price.

It was a wild thought, but he was in a desperate mood. He tramped beside his father down
London Road and worked it out. He'd write to her
tonight, that's what he'd do; bold and desperate as
he now was, he still could not face the thought of
seeing her again.

His father had said nothing to him in the train,
nothing as they went through the Ardwick streets,
but by the way he breathed Willy could tell that

there was going to be much said when the door of 19 Audley Street closed behind them. Once they turned into Audley Street they got a lot of attention. Children stopped their games on the pavement and pointed and called. People looked at them through the lace curtains, and a few of the bolder women on the other side of the road even opened their doors to peer out. "Not in the canal then after all?" shouted one, clutching at an unbuttoned bodice front. "Where did you pick him up then?"

Mr. Overs did not vouchsafe any reply. He strode on to number 19, threw the door open, and pushed Willy in. A familiar blue serge back cumbrously swung around and surveyed them over a yellow-stained, walrus mustache. "Ah," said Mr. Buller, "So you're back."

"He's back, Mr. Buller," said Willy's father, "and I reckon he'll never run away again—not after I've finished with him."

"Willy," said his mother on the other side of the counter, "Willy, how could you have done it?" He could see her now around the bulk of Mr. Buller. He was shocked at her face, her eyes all reddened and sunk, her cheeks blotchy.

"Well, I reckon I'll be going," said Mr. Buller. He lumbered toward the door and was gone.

"Don't you go a kissing and a slobbering over him, Ellen," said Mr. Overs. "He isn't worth it. He doesn't care a straw for us. Been enjoying himself, he has, all the time we was worrying ourselves silly. And then when I tells him the state you was in, all he says is, will I buy him a shop to play with."

"Oh, Willy," said his mother, "you never did?"

Willy stared at her mutely, his face stony. He knew that if he relaxed a muscle, tears would come pouring down his cheeks.

"Oh, Willy. If you knew the state we's been in on account of you. The whole street turned upside down looking for you, and that Mrs. Jericho coming in every half hour to know if you was found. Fair gloating she was, and then came to say that two lads had left the tandem outside in the street, and did we know. It was then I thought I'd never see you again, Willy. I thought they'd done you in. Why couldn't you have told us where you was going, Willy?"

"Because he didn't care, that's why."

"And us sending over to Harold and Kitty to know if you'd gone there. It's the shame of it; I'll never get over it. The whole of Audley Street knows, *and* Harold and Kitty, and we was always so proud of you, Willy."

"Proud, were you? Well, there's no call to be proud of Willy anymore, he's let us down worse than I believed any son of mine could. And what he's been up to in that place we've still got to find out. There was people shouting things at him, and him shouting things back and carrying on like a mad thing all the way to Stockport. We'll have the police knocking on our door before long, I daresay."

"The police, Alfred?" Willy's mother clutched her hand to her mouth. "It'll kill me!"

"There you are," said Mr. Overs with grim satisfaction. "Look what you've done to your mother!"

The door from the parlor opened and George's head poked out. "Is Will all right, then?"

"*He's* all right. It's your mother and me that ain't. He's struck us a mortal blow, has Willy, and we'll never get over it."

To this there seemed nothing that could be said. Willy bit the inside of his lip, lowered his head, and slouched off. You could not just say you were sorry when your father said he would never get over the blow you had struck him. Things had gone too far for that.

"Are you hungry, Willy?" his mother called after him as he went through the parlor door.

"Don't you bother whether he's hungry or not. He's been taking good care of himself, I'll swear to that," shouted his father furiously.

George followed him as he dragged himself up

the dark, steep stairs. Willy took no notice, but when George followed him into their bedroom he rounded on him with clenched fists. Then he relaxed.

"Get me some paper and an envelope and something to write with," Willy said ferociously. "And just you keep quiet that you want it for me or I'll throw it all at you."

George gave him a startled look and scuttled downstairs. He was back soon. "They're still hard at it in the shop," he said with satisfaction. "So I just took this from the kitchen. You haven't half stirred them up, you and your goings on." He heaved himself on to the brass rails at the foot of the bed and sat there eyeing Willy eagerly. "What do you want all that for?"

"You just mind your own business," said Willy savagely. "And clear out."

Left by himself he wrote his letter to Miss Chaffey. The words poured out of him and he flung them down on the paper.

Dear Miss Chaffey,
I write because you are the only person I know who can help. There is an old woman who needs help badly. She lives in the country and keeps a shop but is too old for it. If you

could buy it from her I could go there and look after it for you and I am sure I could make it pay so that it was worth your while. I shall be thirteen in June so I shall be leaving school and I do not want to stay at home any-more. The name of the person who owns the shop is Mrs. Nance Price and she lives at Staseley near Stockport. If you write to her she may not understand, but I could come to you and explain if you like.

I hope you keep well.

Yours faithfully,
William Cobbett Overs

It only took him a few minutes to write. Then, heedless of his parents and George, he let himself out of the backyard, and went to post it.

· *16* ·

Fireworks

He saw no more of his family that day. When he came in, he undressed and climbed into bed—unnatural, it seemed, to be pulling his nightshirt over his head in broad daylight—and turned his head away when George came up to call him down to tea. His mother came up later, he knew her by her tread, but he pretended to be fast asleep. She went away, leaving a plate with a Cornish pasty on it by his bed. For a while he resisted the temptation, but later his hunger grew too much for him, and he sat up and devoured it all. He must have been asleep when George came to bed, for he had no memory at all of him coming in, and was surprised to find him there in the morning.

As he looked at George, he could only see tousled hair, the rest was buried under bedclothes.

George woke, groped his way out, and stared at Willy.

"Cor, you had a long sleep, didn't you? Went to bed before tea. I didn't know people could do that unless they were ill. Are you coming to school this morning?"

School! It was Thursday today, only three days since he was last there, but he felt separated from it by a span of years. "I suppose so," he muttered.

"Well, you'd better look sharp and dress, hadn't you? I say, there are going to be some fireworks, you just wait and see if there aren't."

The home fireworks were going to be reserved until the evening, this much he gathered from what was said at the breakfast table. His father never was much in the kitchen at that hour of the morning anyway; he was busy in the shop sorting out all the newspapers, and Mrs. Overs always took him in cups of tea and bread and marmalade. This morning he came into the kitchen to get another cup. Willy fixed his eyes on his porridge bowl—from which he had eaten very little—and Mrs. Overs, with a falter in her voice, spoke up.

"Now don't go starting, Alfred. The boys are late as it is and there isn't time. You say what you want to say this evening when Willy comes home from school."

"They'll have something to say to him at school, if I'm not mistaken."

The kitchen door banged behind him, and then they heard the parlor door bang. George sucked in his cheeks meaningly and looked sideways at his brother.

"You are going to get it," he remarked with satisfaction as the boys went down Audley Street later on. "The row there's been at school about you!"

Willy had been feverishly turning over in his mind the possible consequences of his appeal to Miss Chaffey. He weighed the phrases he had used, trying to calculate the effect they would have on her and trying to visualize the arrival of the letter at Laurel Villas. He had given no thought to what would happen at school. "School?" he said. "Do they know about it there?"

"What's wrong with you? You've been away since Monday night and you're acting as though everybody goes off and stays away for three days! What've you been doing anyway? You haven't said a word so far and Father's so boiling he'd knock me over if I asked."

Willy ignored all this. "What happened at school?" he asked, remembering bitterly Mr. Church's humiliation at his father's hands.

"Well," George began with gusto, "we spent

most of Monday evening looking for you and asking everyone, and Father went to the police and then to Uncle Harold's. Then the tandem came back, but it only made Mother carry on worse because she thought someone must have done you in. They made me go to bed but they were up all night, I reckon. Then Tuesday they made me go to school, but Father came, too, and he talked to the headmaster and Mr. Church. Then a policeman came. I suppose he went and saw your class. Anyway, he came to ours, right in the middle of arithmetic too. Asked all the boys in turn whether they'd seen William Overs. It lasted until we should have been doing grammar—old Sloppy was nearly busting himself with rage, but he had to keep quiet. It was the best morning we'd ever had. Then when I went home to dinner there was a telegram from you, and Father and Mother trying to work out what it meant. I'd never seen a telegram before. And Father went off to the police again and told me to tell the headmaster and Mr. Church you were safe, and that took up a bit of time as I walked around a bit and told old Sloppy I couldn't find them. So I missed the spelling test. So Tuesday I had hardly any lessons at all," he finished with satisfaction.

A sudden thought struck Willy. "What hap-

pened to the shop when Father was out looking . . ." He could not bring himself to add "for
me," and broke off.

"It was closed up," George said airily. "Mother
couldn't take it on, she was carrying on so."

"Closed up!" repeated Willy. It was then that the
magnitude of what he had done first struck him.
Except for Sundays the shop had been open from
half past eight until half past six every day of his
life. He had never thought there would ever come
a day when his father would shut it up and leave it.

"Yes, that's what he did. Now, where'd I got to?"
George did not often have a story to tell, and he
was making the most of this one. "Oh, yes, Tuesday. Well, Tuesday night was a bit better because
they did know you weren't dead, though Mother
was crying all the time and Father carrying on
alarming about you and your wickedness that he
never would have credited. And Mother saying
you weren't wicked like that and it must be somebody who had took you off, and how long would it
be before the police went to look for you at the
place where you had sent the telegram from.
Wednesday, that's yesterday, I went to school, and
we was all hoping the police would come again in
the middle of long division. Only they didn't and I
was just going home to dinner when somebody
said I was wanted in the headmaster's office, and

he showed me a telegram he said I could take home to Father. Trust him to wait till dinner time. I bet it came earlier and he just hung on to it till lessons were over."

"Who was it from?" demanded Willy. All along he had wondered how his father had got track of him.

"We couldn't make it out who it was from. It just said 'Headmaster, Rutland Street School, Manchester. Boy from your school found in Staseley lodging with Mrs. Price,'" rattled off George, with an air of having repeated it many times already. "And then it said 'de Staseley' and nobody knew what that meant."

But Willy understood. "De Staseley?" he repeated. "It was the earl then!"

"The earl?" said George blankly. "Who's that?"

"He's a lord." Willy was fitting it into place. The earl had been in the village yesterday, and old Mrs. Barnes had been gossiping around the place too. Between them they had run him down and come in and asked Nance Price about him. She had told Willy they had been on at her about Joey.

But George had fastened on the word "lord." "A real lord? Like one of those Father's always carrying on about? What's he got to do with you?"

Willy saw he would have to tell George more, if only to stop his pestering. "I was walking in some woods of his," he said shortly. "He came along and asked me what I was doing and what school I was at. I didn't tell him any more but I reckon he must have asked questions in the village and put things together."

"What were you doing in his woods then?"

"Having a look around."

"Then why did he want to send telegrams about you?"

Willy shrugged. "They're like that. He said I ought to be in school."

"Cor," said George, now completely diverted from his saga. "You talking to a real lord, and him sending telegrams about you. What did he look like?"

"Like Father mostly."

"He didn't!" George's voice was shrill with incredulous disbelief. "No, what did he look like really? Tell us, Will!"

"Like Father, I'm telling you. Ginger whiskers. Sometimes he rode a horse, though."

"Rode a horse!" said George. This was a bit better. They had reached the school gates now, and he charged on into the playground, hot with his news.

Willy was shrinking from the mob shrieking and tumbling around the asphalt. Any second now, he knew, they would spot him and would be falling

on him with their questions. Then he felt a hand
on his shoulder. Looking up with a start, he saw
Mr. Church.

"So you have returned, William?"

Tears welled up in Willy's eyes. He could only
nod.

"Then you had better come inside and explain
matters to the headmaster."

Mr. Church, his hand still on Willy's shoulder,
propelled him through the throngs in the playground, who fell back and stared at him as they
passed. Mr. Church and Willy climbed the steps
and went down the silent stone corridor with its
shiny brown bricks; the hubbub of the playground
became distant shouting. Mr. Church opened a
classroom door. "This appears to be empty. No
doubt we may use this for a moment."

It was one of the infants' classrooms: high,
gaunt, and unnaturally still, smelling heavily of
the Jeyes Fluid with which its floor had just been
swabbed. Pinned toward the lower edge of the
bleak walls were the letters of the alphabet, with
animals to illustrate them. Q q Quagga was the
picture imprinted on Willy's mind afterward,
though at the time he was hardly aware of it.

"I understand you were absent because you ran
away," said Mr. Church.

Willy nodded dumbly.

"Had you any reason for running away?"

Willy took his mind back to Monday. Subsequent events had overshadowed those of that day; it seemed a very long time ago.

"I was angry," he said hanging his head. "I sort of lost my head and was off before I thought."

"You were angry with some other boys?"

"No," he whispered. "With my father." Painfully he remembered Mr. Church's visit to the shop— his father, Mr. Overs, whacking the counter and carrying on about Cobbett and the Northern Star. He shuffled his feet and prayed that Mr. Church would ask no more.

"Yes," said Mr. Church slowly, "you had a disappointment on Monday. I remember that."

Outside a bell was clanging, a door was pulled open, and the muffled shouts of the playground turned into a roar; footsteps were pounding up the steps. Willy thought of all the boys who would be crowding around tormenting him with questions. Perhaps Mr. Church saw him flinch. "You may go upstairs to your classroom now," he said. "I will take it on myself to excuse you from assembly, and I will speak to the headmaster for you."

Mr. Church went even further. He kept Willy inside during the recreation period, and set him to covering books with brown paper. He kept him back for a few minutes after the end of morning school to discuss the work he had missed during the previous two days. The crowds of the curious had dispersed by the time Willy set off home for dinner. He did not see his father at dinner; school hours were not the same as shop hours, and Mr. Overs was never able to come in for his meal until the boys were on their way back for the afternoon lessons.

But nothing Mr. Church could do was going to save him from his father that evening; from that there was no escape—unless he ran away again. The boys got in soon after four, but they had to wait until after half past six, when Mr. Overs, having locked up the shop, came down the hallway for his tea. The table had been laid, but Willy had turned back a corner of the cloth, and had spread his geometry book there and was working out a problem. He kept his eyes fixed on the diagram when his father came in.

"Well," said Mr. Overs heavily, "you've deigned to come back, have you? And what did they say to you at school, eh?" He pulled out his chair and sat down.

"Have a bite to eat first, Alfred," said Mrs. Overs anxiously. "It's stew, and it ought to be ate before it's cold." She put a plate down before him and in front of George. "You put away your work now, Willy, you've been at it long enough."

Her hands were trembling, and her movements were stiff and fumbling so that gravy from the stew was spilled on the tablecloth. Mr. Overs sawed savagely at the meat and thrust his fork into it as if it were an enemy.

"If you're expecting to put me off forever from speaking my mind to Willy, Ellen, then you're wrong. We're having this out just as soon as tea is cleared off the table—and there's a lot to be said, I can tell you."

After that, nothing was said for a long time. The clatter of knives and forks sounded unnaturally loud, and Mr. Overs seemed to be slamming down the salt and pepper-pots with ferocious violence. Into this atmosphere loaded with unspoken bitterness, George plunged. He was never one for tact or for thinking ahead, so there is no knowing whether he knew what he was up to.

"Father, you know that peculiar name at the end of the telegram they sent the school about Willy? Where we didn't know if the post office had been mistook or not?"

"Do you think I won't forget that telegram till my dying day?"

"De something or other, the same as the name of the place, it was. Well, Willy says that it's the name of a lord!"

There was silence; it was taking a moment or two for Willy's parents to work this out. George was disappointed at the lack of response. "A lord!" he repeated. "An aristocrat like the ones Father carries on about! He saw Willy hanging around and sent to the school to fetch him away!"

A bit of mutton fell off Mr. Overs' fork. "Do you mean to tell me, Willy Overs, that I'm beholden to an aristocrat for rescuing my own son and bringing him back to me?"

Willy abandoned all pretense at eating, laid down his knife and fork, and clenched his hands under the table, twisting the cloth around his fingers.

"Who is this man, this de Staseley or whatever he's called? What's he got to do with you?"

"You saw him," said Willy into the table, "on the horse."

"That fellow? Him with the ginger whiskers and the voice like a donkey braying and a glass that he stuck in his eye? Well now, all along I've wanted to know just what there was between you and him and what you was doing groveling in the dust in front of him, and what he said when he was passing which I was so put out that I didn't fully hear. So just you start to explain; all this has waited too long."

Willy said nothing, but twisted the tablecloth with such strength that his plate was dragged perilously near the edge.

"Well, Willy Overs, I'm waiting."

"It was Lord de Staseley," said Willy, talking into his lap. "I went walking in woods that belonged to him, and he found me there and said I ought to be in school and what school did I go to and where was I staying. And I told him and I suppose he sent a telegram."

"Then what did he mean by talking about books? Though isn't it just what I've always been on and on at you about till I'm sick and weary, that books get you nowhere. I suppose it's all them you got out of the library as has made you turn out like this. Though I never thought I'd have a lord telling me this about my own son."

"It wasn't that sort of book at all," said Willy with fierce indignation.

"Then what was it?"

Too late Willy realized the trap he had fallen into. "It was a book Mrs. Price gave me. But I didn't read it. They pulled it out of my pocket."

"Pulled it out of your pocket—as if you'd been a common thief! Well, what was it?"

"It was called something like *Flash Jim the Cracksman*," said Willy after a long pause. "But I didn't read it, truly I didn't."

"But you was going to, if you hadn't been picked up. The sort of muck you know I'd never allow over the doorsill, and as soon as you get away from home you make a grab at it."

"And you who's always been brought up so careful!" moaned his mother. "Not like the rest of them in the street."

"And of all the people who has to tell me about what you've done, it has to be a busybody with a handle to his name—one of that lot that's never done a hand's turn for anybody, but bloated himself on the pickings of the country. It's him, a lily-livered parasite, that has to tell a decent Manchester man who's always worked for his living, and earned his food honorably, and his father and his grandfather before him. It's him that has to tell me that my own son's no good."

"But I tell you I didn't even look at it!" shouted Willy. "I'd forgotten it was even there and I wouldn't have looked at it either. I don't read stuff like that. It's baby stuff. I read the things Mr. Church tells me to get from the library. And I tell you you're wrong, all your things about lords. You've never talked to one, I have. They don't parasite, it's the other way, they go around—" He searched his mind wildly for something that would convey what the earl had said about the way he concerned himself with the local people. "They go around being a father to all the people on their property—and that means interfering, like you do with me. And what's more, he looks like you, this one does."

A stunned silence met this outburst. It was a completely new departure at Audley Street, for either of the boys to contradict their father, let alone with this violence, and on Mr. Overs' own pet subject too. Then Mrs. Overs raised her voice. Most of what Willy had said seemed to have passed her by, it was the calumny about the book that was grieving her now.

"Well, if you didn't read it and didn't know what it was you had, Willy, why didn't you tell him so?"

"I did," said Willy angrily. "But he wouldn't listen. Too fond of his own speechifying—like Father," he added bitterly.

"And now he'll go to his grave thinking that you were one of that nasty low sort from the other side of the road that reads heaven knows what if they read at all. And he'll never know that you were brought up strict and go to chapel regular." Mrs. Overs was crying now. "Why didn't *you* tell him, Alfred? You said you saw him, you could have told him the sort of boy our Willy was!"

Mr. Overs, deflated and uneasy, looked at her

uncomfortably. "You can't tell people like that anything. Besides, I didn't know what he was on about, he didn't give me a chance, just rode past."

Mrs. Overs' shoulders were now heaving with her sobs, and it was difficult to hear what she was saying. "Somebody ought to tell him then, and if you don't, I will," she asserted from behind her handkerchief.

Mr. Overs gave a dismayed look at the boys, half rose out of his chair as if he were going to comfort her, thought better of it, and sat down and cleared his throat. "You've no call to do anything of the sort," he said at last. "It's Willy's affair, and he must do it himself. Yes, you, Willy. Right now. I'm not having that fellow going around with wrong ideas about the Overs for a second longer than I can help it."

Mrs. Overs raised her head. "You'll do it, Willy? You'll write a nice letter to the lord and tell him that you're not at all the sort of boy he thought you was, and that you know how to behave and that you've never been allowed to have that sort of book?"

"He'll do what he's told to do," said Mr. Overs sharply. "You just get out the ink and some paper, Willy, and write that letter straight away. Then you can take it up to the station so's it catches tonight's post. And you just send him the money for that telegram of his. I'm not going to be beholden to any aristocrat. There's stamps in the till, you can take a shillings worth—no, one and six to be on the safe side."

· 17 ·

MISS CHAFFEY'S SUMMONS

It is difficult to write a letter working against time with all your family staring at you, and in any case, Willy was exhausted by the emotions of the last few days. He wrote the address and the date on the paper that his mother found for him, then hesitated, chewing the top of the pen.

"No nonsense about giving him fancy titles," said his father fiercely. "You're not a slave to lick his boots. You call him 'dear sir' same's anyone else."

The letter that Willy produced disappointed him, it sounded bald and much too simple. He would have liked time to work out something really eloquent.

Dear Sir (it read),
    I write to say that I am the boy who was

staying with Mrs. Price. When I came in your woods I did not know they were yours; I apologize. The book that you found in my pocket was put there by Mrs. Price. I would not have touched it if I had known what it was as I scorn books of that sort. I read books about history and music which I borrow from the library. You did not give me a chance to speak otherwise I would have told you. I am sorry I trespassed but I did not know that the country belonged to private people.

He got this down fairly quickly and then hesitated again. There was much more he wanted to put, but he needed time to think it out.

"Come on," said his father impatiently. "You aren't writing poetry, you're writing a business letter and the time's coming when you'll be writing a score of 'em a day. All that schooling hasn't done much if you can't write a letter."

It was that that did it. Willy jammed his pen into the ink pot and set to it again.

In my opinion people who own that amount of land would do better to look after the poor people around them instead of interfering with those who come on by mistake. I mean Mrs. Price, who needs care and has nobody to look after her. My father tells me to send you the money for the cost of the telegram, and I am sending a shilling for you to give to Mrs. Price because I borrowed this to send a telegram to my father.

Yours faithfully,
William Cobbett Overs

His father reached out his hand for the letter when it was done. Willy gave it to him defiantly. "I'll pay back the other shilling," he said, "but can I have the extra stamps now?"

Mr. Overs read it through slowly, then handed it back. "You can take the stamps that are there. That should be enough."

"Does it say that Willy's been brought up nicely and he comes from a nice home?" asked Mrs. Overs with a catch in her voice.

"There's no time for fiddle-faddle of that sort. It tells that earl or whoever he is that he made a mistake. And it puts him right—puts him into his place, you might say," said Mr. Overs with what sounded like a tinge of reluctant approval. "Now get your stamps, Willy, and be off. You post it in the letterbox at the station, then we'll know he gets it first thing tomorrow. George, you go along with him seeing how it's dark."

Mrs. Overs followed Willy into the shop. "Willy," she said in a low voice, shutting the parlor door behind her. "Father's a bit hasty. I wouldn't want them to think we didn't know how to write. 'Dear Sir' doesn't sound right, not to a lord."

"But I can't write it all out again!" protested Willy.

"No, but you could just add a bit," she said pleadingly. "Put 'Dear Sir' and then 'Your Honor.' That sounds more respectful like. It would show you've had schooling, that you're not one of that rough lot that doesn't know how to behave." So "Dear Sir, Your Honor," was the final version that went into the envelope along with the stamps.

"Have you got that book, *Flash Jim*, or whatever it's called?" said George hungrily as they panted down London Road.

"No, I haven't."

"Was it really all that bad?"

"I tell you, I never looked inside. It got taken from me before I'd even seen it," snapped Willy.

"It's lucky Father doesn't know half the things *I've* read. The boys at school have them, we read them in class sometimes when old Sloppy's writing things on the board. *The Daring of Dandy Dick*— that was a good one, only I never got a chance to finish it. Sloppy turned around and caught Len

Higgs with his nose in it and tore it up and caned Len. Trust old Len to get caught like that. If I'd had it I wouldn't have been caught, I bet you. I say, you didn't half stand up to Father. You'll be like Uncle Harold one of these days. You ought to be a school teacher, that's what you ought to be, always with your nose in a book and bellowing away like that."

The streets were empty and still, and George, behaving as though he was newly released from school, ran and jumped and whooped past the shuttered shops and the blank, staring windows of the dark blocks of offices that lined the city end of London Road.

"The Northern Star, Will!" he called out over his shoulder. "You'll be there soon. Perhaps you'll be walking down to the shop to buy your cigars. The pavement will be fair wore out by your footsteps by the time you've finished. Does the Northern Star have a buzzer to call you to work?"

Willy had had enough. Catching up to George, he clumped him between the shoulders. George gave a howl. "You aren't half in a rage these days. Aren't you ever going to stop?"

"Not until you stop acting like a fool."

"Well, I don't know what's wrong with what I said," said George sulkily. "Can't a fellow talk?"

But he sobered down now, and they walked back in silence. It was not until they turned into Audley Street that George spoke again. There was no one about, their boots rang through the stillness, and their shadows went ahead of them, long and black on the lamplit pavements. Then George grabbed at Willy's arm.

"I say, Will, do you see that old body there—do you think she's a witch?"

In the shadows halfway down Audley Street there was certainly a lurking figure—impossible to see whether it was man or woman. "Or perhaps it's a spook," chattered on George. "Bert Andrews lent me a book called *The Spook with the Bloody Hand* once. Only it wasn't a spook at all, it turned out to be smugglers. Come on, let's creep up on this one and see whether it's a spook or not."

But before they got there the figure had disappeared. George stopped and pulled at Willy's coat. "Do you know," he said in a voice that now sounded almost frightened, "I think it's gone into the shop."

They went up the street, George leaning against Willy and scrutinizing each doorway as though he expected somebody to jump out at him. The nearer to number 19 they got, the slower his steps dragged.

"There's a light on in the shop," he said with an air of relief. "Father must be there still, tidying up or something."

He pushed the door open, and stopped dead with a startled exclamation. Peering over his shoulder, Willy saw Hannah Raffetty. All along he had thought it would be Hannah. She was wearing the same rusty clothes that he remembered, and the squashed bonnet on her head, now at a tipsy angle, as though it had slipped there after long months of living in it, day and night. Behind the counter, visibly ill at ease and apprehensive, stood Mr. Overs.

"Willy," he said, in a low voice. "It's Auntie Maggie—she wants us to go."

"Go where?" said Willy. But he knew. He had been expecting the summons.

"Am I going too?" George asked, staring at Hannah Raffetty.

"Quiet, George, I don't want your mother disturbed. No, you stay here and keep her company."

"Miss Chaffey said particular that *she* was to come too." Hannah Raffetty peered forward scrutinizing the boys. "And this one ain't the one she meant, neither," she said, indicating George, who, unable to make out what was going on, turned and stared at Willy. Hannah Raffetty screwed up her face and contemplated Willy, who was still lurking in the background.

"Ay, that's the one. All boys look the same to me, but he's got the hair that sticks up, like she said. Come on now, we'd best be moving, there's been enough delay as it is."

"Go and get my coat from the hallway, George," commanded Mr. Overs. "And if your mother asks where I am say it's all right, and I've just gone out with Willy for a bit. Mrs. Overs won't be coming," he said defiantly to Hannah Raffetty. "She's in delicate health, and I won't answer for the consequences if she hears a word about all this."

"And I won't answer for what the old woman'll do to you when she hears. Still, you'll have to do the talking, not me."

As Willy followed his father and Hannah Raffetty through the streets he felt sick with apprehension. It was too late now to wish that letter had never been written; once again the wheel was sweeping forward with him on it. At the end of Grosvenor Street they got on one of the trams that went down the Wilmslow Road. Nobody said anything until they had left it and were walking down High Street. Then Mr. Overs cleared his throat.

"Did Miss Chaffey say why it was she wanted to see us?"

"It's her will. She says she wants to make a new will. Reckon she must have fallen out with them fat lot from Trafford. Never took to them much meself, too much beef and bluster, I say, for all they hang around her like sucking toads."

"Then is she feeling . . . poorly?" hesitated Mr. Overs, ". . . late at night like this and all?"

"If you mean has she been took bad and wants to say good-bye? Well, no, she's the same as usual. It's just her nature to put people to as much trouble as she knows how."

As soon as they moved into the circle of light thrown by the gas lamp outside Laurel Villas, there was a frenzy of rapping on the window. Willy, who had been keeping well apart from his father, now stole a glance at him and moved a bit closer. It all painfully recalled the hideous nightmares of his illness.

"That's how I knew it'd be," remarked Hannah Raffetty. "And she'll probably have the glass out when she sees your ma ain't here."

She led the way up the garden path, produced an enormous key from a pocket and opened the door. The damp cold air rushed out to meet them, and the darkness that lay within looked impenetrable.

"You'll have to wait till I find the candle. Don't

you go treading about till I've lit up, there's a ceiling come down last week, and I haven't got around to clearing it up yet."

From the bottom of the passage came the snarling of dogs and a gnawing, rending sound. "Them devil dogs at it again." Hannah Raffetty picked up the feeble flame she had just lit and went down the hall, leaving Willy and his father standing in the pitch darkness by the front door. "Give over, will you!" she shouted, banging at the door. The snarls turned to savage barking, and there was a sound of claws scrabbling on the wood.

The wan, pale flame came up the passage toward them. Willy could see where the ceiling had fallen now, with a heap of rubble near the foot of the stairs, and a gaping black hole overhead. Behind the door the scraping and gnawing had begun again.

"What are they doing in there?" Mr. Overs asked, edging his way gingerly past the rubble.

"Them's her guard dogs, keeps the thieves from her money. And while they waits for the thieves they eats the rot. The floorboards is rotten, like all the house, like all of us here, come to that, and the dogs tears away at it and eats it. There'll be a day when they'll eat their way out of the house, and where we'll be then I'm sure I don't know. Dead and buried, maybe, I don't know. Do you reckon the place has changed since you was here?"

They were mounting the stairs now, feeling their way up in the darkness. "She hasn't gone to much trouble to keep it up, has she?" said Mr. Overs after long hesitation.

Mrs. Raffetty gave a grim laugh. "Keeping it up! The only thing what's been kept up is me, kept on my legs the whole time since you two went your ways and left her. And now she's asked for you back again, after all she said. Well, wonders will never cease, they say. Though it could be because of a letter she got this morning." She paused meaningly, and Willy's heart gave a jump that seemed to take it almost out of his body. "Would you or Miss Ellen have been writing?" Hannah Raffetty whispered hoarsely. They were up on the landing now.

"Certainly not," said Mr. Overs fiercely.

There was a muffled shout from behind the door opposite. "Hannah Raffetty, you stop your whispering and plotting, I can hear you out there. You send 'em in."

Willy and his father stood by the door of Miss Chaffey's room, peering into the gloom. Firelight threw flickering shadows on the ceiling, otherwise the only light came from a candle by the bed at the far end. There, sitting up, silhouetted against the uncurtained window, sat Miss Chaffey, her face turned toward them.

"Come on, come on," she screeched. "Don't stand hovering there. I can't abide folks that hover. One thing about that lot from Trafford, they don't hover, they comes marching over as bold as brass. And it's my brass they're after, ain't they just." She gave a cracked laugh. "But they ain't going to have it. Oh, no, I've made up my mind, and I've called to tell you so. Come along, I want to see you after all these years."

Mr. Overs was edging his way through the welter of furniture, Willy keeping close behind. Miss Chaffey peered up at him. "Alfred Overs, eh? Well, you never thought to see me again, did you? Well, don't go standing blocking out the others! Where's the rest of you?"

Willy slunk forward and stood beside his father, looking down at the shriveled figure in the bed. "Where's Ellen?" Miss Chaffey leaned forward and scrutinized the shadowy room. "What've you done with Ellen? I sent for her particular. If that Hannah Raffetty hasn't brought her I'll . . ."

"Ellen stayed behind," said Mr. Overs loudly. "It's my doing. She's been very upset this week, and I wasn't going to have her upset again."

"So it's you who've kept her from me, is it? You who took her away in the first place. Took her to a place in Ardwick with two rooms up and two down. It was a bad day when I let her go to that Sacred Song Festival in Grosvenor Street Wesleyan and she took up with you. And I suppose it was you who put the boy onto me."

"Put the boy onto you?" repeated Mr. Overs. "What boy?"

"That boy." Miss Chaffey pointed a skinny, trembling finger in Willy's direction. "Sent him to stand outside my house, made him write a letter to me."

Mr. Overs turned to stare incredulously at Willy. "I don't reckon to know anything about his goings on these days," he said heavily. "He's cut himself off from us, he has. He's heard nothing about you from us, that I can tell you. Your name hasn't so much as been spoke in Audley Street in Willy's or George's presence."

Miss Chaffey gave a sudden cackle. "Cut himself off from you, has he? He's a nice little fellow, a proper Chaffey, he knows his place isn't in Ardwick, don't you, my duck?"

But Willy shuddered and cowered in his father's shadow.

"You're a good boy, you don't want to have anything to do with that Ardwick lot, do you? You want to leave home, that's what you said, didn't you?" Even by the dim light of the candle that stood on the table beside her Willy could see the triumphant look she gave his father. "There's no one else that can help you, you say, no one but Auntie Maggie. That's right, isn't it?"

But Willy still said nothing. Put like this it sounded quite different from what he had meant. He pulled at the cap he was clutching and looked down at the pools of darkness on the floor.

"Well," said Miss Chaffey impatiently. "You tell your father that you don't like a sweet shop with two up and two down any more than I did."

But Mr. Overs found his voice before Willy did. "I don't know what's been going on behind my back. I suppose as being only Willy's father I haven't any right even to ask. But I can tell you this, in case Willy hasn't condescended to, that we have given a great deal of thought to his future. We never meant him to stay in the shop. Willy's good enough to make his way to high places. We're going to put him in the insurance business. There's opportunities for bright lads there. Mr. Ramsbottom of the Northern Star comes to the shop regular; he's going to find Willy a place."

There was a silence. Then Miss Chaffey heaved

herself up in the bed and seized the candle and held it in Willy's direction. "And what do you think about Mr. Ramsbottom of the Northern Star who comes to the shop regular? What do you think about the place he's going to find you? You don't look as if you're jumping for joy."

Mention of the Northern Star roused Willy. Memories of his long dread of the place, his hatred of Mr. Ramsbottom and his codfish eyes, fanned his rebellion into new flames.

"I don't want to go to the Northern Star," he said loudly. "It's a prison. I want to look after that shop for Mrs. Price, that's all I want to do."

"Well, we must help you get out of your prison, mustn't we," said Miss Chaffey gloatingly. "Where's that place you want to escape to, eh?"

"It's called Staseley," said Willy lamely, the fire dying out of him now. "It's a little place the other side of Stockport."

"And you want me to buy a shop there so's you can run it?"

"It wasn't because of me running it so much as old Mrs. Price being able to be comfortable," muttered Willy.

"Oh, yes, we understand what that means. Come along, come nearer, you're a Chaffey, don't forget, and it's not often I see one."

Reluctantly Willy shuffled a few steps forward. She reached forward and grabbed at his arm with a clawlike hand. He could feel the heat from the candle flame on his face.

"There now, that's right. Now do you see what I've got here?" She lowered the candle so that Willy could make out some bundles lying on the bedspread. "Bank notes! Some puts their faith in gold, but not me! I like the rustle of good paper, and I like the words that's written on it! Now then, supposing I was to give you a hundred pounds now, and write it into my will that you was to have everything, then you could go off and leave that Ardwick lot, couldn't you? You could buy that little place in the country and you could set up and be a Chaffey. And you could tell 'em all that a Chaffey gave you the money, and it's a Chaffey that you are. Why, you could paint 'Chaffey' on that little place that you want to buy!"

Her grip tightened on his arm, and she drew him nearer. Appalled, Willy stared back at the face poking out of the shadows.

"Well," crooned the voice, "you don't seem none too grateful. That Trafford lot would be jumping up and down for joy; they've never been as close to my money as you are, though they've been trying for it all these years. You're going to be William

Chaffey, aren't you, my duck? Not William Overs anymore."

"No," he shouted, wrenching away his arm. "I don't want anything from you. I shouldn't ever have written, it was wrong. And I'm not a Chaffey, I'll have you know. My name is Overs, like Father's, and I want to stay in Ardwick with Father and Mother."

Somehow he got out of the room, and down the stairs, only to crash headlong over the pile of plaster in the hall. It was his father who picked him up, brushed him down and took him into the street.

"I didn't mean it to be like that, Father," he kept saying incoherently as his father led him down High Street. "I only wanted to help old Mrs. Price, but she got it all wrong."

"She's a wicked woman, Willy. She tried to split your mother and me apart but we wasn't having any of that. And now she's trying it on you."

"She won't get me to go, I promise you. I promise I'll never see her anymore. I don't want to leave you and Mother and George—ever."

· *18* ·

THE OVERS ON TOP

It had taken Miss Chaffey, it seemed, to restore Audley Street to a state of peace. Not that there was any formal reconciliation between Willy and his father, but even as they walked home wearily up Oxford Street, Willy knew that things were back on the old footing. They spoke very little during that trudge through the dark and deserted streets. It was late by now, past ten o'clock; a couple of trams still clattered down Oxford Street, drawn by horses who knew that the load was light and that they were on their way home. A few tipsy revelers were reeling out of the Ardwick pubs and bawling into the silence. Otherwise, Manchester seemed asleep. Mr. Overs took Willy's arm after a bit, and Willy whose steps had been flagging, did not pull it away. In fact, he edged closer.

And by the next day, though nothing had been said so far as Willy knew, the peace had spread to his mother and to George and everybody was behaving as they always used to. Except that his mother seemed extra solicitous, and he came down the next morning to find her frying ham for him.

"You were up so late last night, it must have taken a lot out of you," she said. "It's a good thing it's Friday today and the weekend ahead. Not but what it isn't first Sunday and our turn."

"Still, there'll be a good spread," said George. "Lucky Father got Will back in time—there would be a rumpus if we still couldn't find him. Can I have ham too? I was out with Will when it was quite late."

That was all that was said about the last few days, and characteristically, it was George who said it. When Willy came home that afternoon from school his mother's mind seemed to be on other things—nor was it the preparation of Sunday's tea. He found her ironing, the kitchen full of the smell of hot, damp cloth; she looked up from the table with a flushed face and pushed back a strand of hair.

"It's your trousers. I thought I'd just give them a press for the Northern Star tomorrow. Father's fixed it that he's going to take you at half past twelve. It's a bit awkward about the shop, seeing as how I'll be busy with first Sunday, but I daresay we'll get by somehow." She gave Willy what seemed almost a nervous look, and then bent hastily to the ironing again. "I did start to give your shoes a bit of a polish, too, but maybe you'd like to rub them up yourself. Father wants you to look nice and I always say it takes a man to polish properly. But sit down and have a cake first, I've just taken them out of the oven and they're still hot."

Usually there was nothing of this sort during first Sunday preparations, and a currant cake hot from the oven would be a treat at the best of times. Three were put on a plate for him, and Willy sat and ate them in silence. It was good to be eating his mother's food again, and sitting in a place where everything was scrubbed and burnished, and even the floor where the range stood was stoned to dazzling whiteness. When he had finished he picked the crumbs from his jacket front—fresh cakes make a lot of crumbs—stood up and went over to the door. His mother paused with a flat iron in her hand.

"Where are you going?" Her voice sounded anxious.

"Just to shine up my boots," he said.

Mrs. Overs dropped the iron with a clatter onto the stand, and came running over to the door. She was still clutching the ironholder with its red gingham cover as she put her hands on his shoulders and kissed him.

"Oh, Willy." There were tears in her voice. "I knew all along it would be all right. You're a good lad, Willy."

As he rubbed away at his boots in the scullery he wondered whether leaving them unpolished would mean that the Northern Star wouldn't take him, and whether, if so, it might not have been a good plan to leave them scuffed. He sighed, and rubbed harder.

"Cor," said George, coming in a few minutes later to splash his hands under the sink tap. "You aren't half getting a shine. That for old fishface Ramsbottom? You must want that job bad. Though I'd want a job bad if it meant I could leave school. Do you know what old Sloppy did today? Kept the lot of us back after school just because Bert Andrews had thrown a piece of chalk at someone. It didn't even hit anyone either. You know what old Bert is like for aim."

They played Beggar My Neighbor after tea with the sticky old cards that they had used ever since Willy could remember, but which had not been produced for months now. Willy had the feeling that his parents were watching him as if they were worrying about him.

"I think I'll go up now," he said at last. "I'm a bit tired."

"That's right, Willy," said Mr. Overs heartily. "You want to be your best for tomorrow. It's a pity you didn't win more cards tonight, though. I'd have liked you to win, just as a sign to show us some of the great things you're going to do when you're started—eh, Willy?"

"I didn't *want* to win," he said heatedly. "I hate winning. Taking everybody's cards like that."

"The trouble with old Will is that he never wants to win anything," said George sagely. "He ought to try and be a thruster like Uncle Harold. I bet you Uncle Harold would win the lot if we played with him. But all Will wants to win is prizes for lessons. He'll never be a thruster."

"Now don't you go teasing Willy," said Mrs. Overs hastily. "He does very well. And he didn't win tonight because he's tired. So he's very sensible to go to bed early. You run along, Willy, and as a special treat I'll bring you a mug of cocoa in bed."

She continued her pampering when it came to next morning's breakfast. There was not only ham, there were eggs, two of them, as well as the usual porridge. And a piece of fried bread to the bargain.

"There's nothing like starting on a full stomach," she said when Willy stared at the plate in front of him. "Makes you feel ready for anything."

Willy doubted very much whether anything could make him feel ready for the Northern Star, and he was certainly not ready to tackle this. In fact he felt rather sick. The knife and fork felt unnaturally heavy and awkward in his hands as he pushed an egg around the plate and cut the white into tiny strips.

"He doesn't want it," announced George. "Look how he's fiddling around with it. Cor, I'll eat it, Will. I bet you I need it more than you, I'm going to play football."

"You just leave him alone," commanded Mrs. Overs. "He'll eat it if you let him be."

"Can I have it, Will?" whispered George hungrily. Willy nodded, and with a sly look at Mrs. Overs who was now standing at the range with her back turned, George speared first the ham, then the eggs, disposing of them in a few gulps.

"You can't eat the fried bread? Well, perhaps it is rather sickly stuff." Mrs. Overs swept the plate away from Willy's place. "Still, you've had a good meal. Now, Father's busy until quarter past twelve, and then he'll be ready to go out with you.

What are you going to do till then? I'll be busy baking. You can sit in the parlor and play the piano if you want. Or in here, if you keep out of my way."

These were concessions indeed. Normally, Willy was not supposed to play the piano during shop hours, nor could Mrs. Overs tolerate anybody around while she was baking. But though Willy appreciated how special these offers were, he did not feel tempted. He wanted to get out of the house rather than stay in it.

"I think I'll go to the library," he said limply. "I've got some books due back."

"All right, you go along, you've got plenty of time. But don't put on your clean boots yet, will you, and be back here by twelve o'clock, there's a good boy, or Father'll be fretting."

"I'll be back before then," he said.

There was a sound of leather smacking against the walls of the back entry and scuffling feet. George and his friends were playing football there.

"Come on, Will, come and have a kick!" yelled George when Willy let himself out through the yard door. But Willy shook his head and plodded on.

It was ten minutes' walk to the library, but by loitering and dragging his feet he turned it into a quarter of an hour. Even so, it left him with hours on his hands. He was the only person in the library. The two men who stamped the books and took the cards were standing by the rusty black coke stove in the center of the room, murmuring to each other. They took little notice of Willy as he trod over the creaking wood floor and wandered from bookcase to bookcase. The trouble was he could not concentrate, nor think of anything that he particularly wanted to read. He pulled out volume after volume and flicked through the pages and replaced them without the remotest idea of what they had said. His mind was not on them at all, it was on the Northern Star and what lay ahead of him. Ten minutes of today's time, fifteen perhaps, but a lifetime after that. A lifetime of struggling up that ladder that Father talked about and trying to be like one of Smiles' heroes. And then he might turn into somebody like Mr. Ramsbottom at the end, if he was lucky. Still, better to belong to Mr. Ramsbottom than to Miss Chaffey. He dismissed Miss Chaffey, it was far too unpleasant a subject to dwell on, and he felt ashamed of the way he had been drawn to her. But then there was Nance Price. What had become of her? Was she still standing in all the turmoil and muddle of her cottage, waiting for Joey to come back again? He let the book he was holding fall down against

his side and stared blankly at the iron flue pipe
rearing up into the roof from the cylindrical fluted
stove that always looked as though it had been
meant for a church. Then he became aware that
the clerks had stopped talking and had wheeled
around and were contemplating him with curiosity. Blushing, he hurried to conceal himself behind
a bookcase.

When he eventually left, it was with three books
that he felt he would never read. One was about
mountaineering, one was Prescott's *Conquest of
Peru*, and the third was Macaulay's *Essays*. But then
he knew he could stay there a lifetime and never
find a word that would interest him in his present
mood.

He still had plenty of time on hand, so he daw-
dled around the streets, exploring an area around
Rusholme Road that he had never been in before.
But though he looked around him, it was with
vacant eyes, and afterward he could not remember a single detail.

Eventually he wandered home, thinking that if
George was still playing with his friends he might
join in this time. Even from Crown Street he could
hear the thump of the ball bouncing on the cobbles and the boys' shouts. But when he got up to
the far end, George was not there. Shifting the

books from arm to arm he stood watching the five or six boys who were skirmishing outside the gate to the yard.

"If it's your brother you're looking for, he's gone in," somebody called to him at last. "Folks came to visit your house."

"Came to visit—*us!*" repeated Willy. It was unbelievable that anybody should come visiting; such a thing had never happened before.

"That's what your mum said. Come on, Ted, shove it down here." And the game went on.

Willy went through the yard gate, and up the steps into the house. The kitchen door was open. No one was in there, and the way the rolling pin and the patty tins and the bits of pastry lay strewn on the table suggested that his mother had been called away in a hurry. He could hear voices in the parlor, and went up to see. But he hesitated outside first—supposing it was the police or somebody from Staseley?

The voice speaking now was a female one, though, and within a second or two he placed it as Auntie Kitty's.

"Of course it's not my proper mourning. I called in at Kendal Milne on the way to see about that for me and the girls, while Harold and Stan went on down to High Street. Harold says we must do it proper, it's only respectful, he says, with everything left to Stan. You know everything's left to Stan, don't you? She's often shown Harold her will with that in it. Very fond of him she was. Stan used to go and see her most Saturdays and they got on a fair treat. There's something very taking about our Stan, don't you think? Not that your Willy isn't a nice lad, too, but a bit over quiet. It's a pity she never saw Willy, but she took on so after . . ."

But at this point Willy pushed open the door and went into the parlor. Facing him on the sofa, dressed in black, with a handkerchief trailing out of one hand sat Auntie Kitty. On either side, limply leaning against her, were Lily and Dolly whose eyes wandered vacantly around the room. George had his legs wound around the hard, upright chair that Mr. Overs usually took, and Mrs. Overs sat with her back to the door. There was something rather dejected in the way her shoulders drooped. Hearing Willy behind her, she turned. She, too, was holding a handkerchief and he could see her eyes were red.

"Oh, Willy . . ." she began.

"Miss Chaffey's dead," he said, staring at Auntie Kitty.

"Willy knows about Auntie then!" His aunt showed disappointment. "However did he know?

I always understood you and Alfred weren't telling your boys nothing—letting them think Auntie passed away before you was married. George didn't seem to know."

"I'm sure I don't know, Kitty. I could never bring myself to talk about Auntie, dear knows." And Mrs. Overs put her handkerchief to her eyes.

"Perhaps Stan told," piped up Dolly.

"I found out for myself," said Willy, staring straight at George who had opened his mouth as if to speak, and then catching Willy's eye, had shut it again. "It was an accident, she saw me out of the window and recognized me."

"Recognized you?" He had succeeded in getting Auntie Kitty's attention as never before. In fact, he had never seen her attention caught by anything. "She'd never seen you, how could she recognize you?"

"She said she knew I was a Chaffey just by seeing me through the window."

"She never!" Auntie Kitty was now gaping at him, stripped, for the first time in his memory, of her fine company manners. "You talked to her then?"

"Oh, yes." He was enjoying himself. "Two or three times."

"Did she ever talk to you about any will?" Auntie Kitty asked with an air of nonchalance.

"Yes, she did."

Mrs. Overs had now turned herself around in her chair and was staring at him aghast. As for Auntie Kitty, she had quite forgotten her usual superiority and air of condescension. "Auntie talked to *you* about her will!" She was sitting on the edge of the sofa, quite tense with agitation.

"On Thursday night she did. Father was there," Willy added casually.

"So that's where you were," breathed his mother.

On the sofa Auntie Kitty was losing all restraint. She had got her handkerchief twisted around her fingers and was breathing hard. She had just opened her mouth for more questions when the door from the shop burst open and Mr. Overs appeared, looking strangely excited.

"There's a letter come by second post," he began.

But Auntie Kitty had no time for anything but the matter that was consuming her. "Alfred, Willy says you've been seeing Auntie and she's been talking about her will."

Mr. Overs' attention was on something quite different. "Yes, she said Willy looked a proper Chaffey and she wanted to leave him all her property. Now just you listen to this!"

"But it was Stan's money!" shrieked Auntie

Kitty, falling back against the cushion behind. "She promised!"

This time Mr. Overs ignored her. "Just you listen to this!" He held up a sheet of paper, twirled his mustache, and coughed. "'Dear Mr. Overs,'" he read. "'Dear Mr. Overs,' you mark that, not 'Dear Sir.' 'Dear Mr. Overs, I have today received a letter from your son, a remarkably well-written letter for a lad of his age, and a tribute to our national system of education, in which I and all my family have always taken so deep an interest. I desire to acknowledge the sum which you sent to reimburse the cost of various telegrams, and must commend the scrupulous manner in which you and your son discharge your debts. Please thank your son for the interest he has taken in one of my tenants, and inform him that a place has been found for Mrs. Price in the De Staseley almshouses. I have myself handed over to her the sum of one shilling as your son desired. I beg to remain yours faithfully, De Staseley.'" Mr. Overs drew a deep breath. "What do you think of that for a letter from a lord? De Staseley, that means Lord de Staseley, Kitty. Willy's been having dealings with him. 'A remarkably well-written letter for a lad of his age,' he says. And you should see the coat of arms on the envelope. You could have knocked me down with a feather when the postman came in with it."

"It's a pity, though, he didn't say nothing about being mistaken over Willy reading that book," said Mrs. Overs. But you could tell she was pleased all the same.

"I don't think you ought to be talking of things like this when Auntie's dead only a mile or two away," said her sister reprovingly.

"Auntie, ah, yes," said Mr. Overs jovially, "took a real fancy to Willy, she did. Like this lord did. Very like me, Willy said he was, and I think he's right there. You should have seen Willy standing up to him. Jumped out of the trap on the way home that day and went for him. That's what they like, these aristocrats, to be stood up to."

Auntie Kitty sucked in her breath with a hiccuping sound, buried her face in her handkerchief, and began to sob. "Talking like this when Auntie's dead and hardly cold! And her so fond of Stan and all of us. And if she changed her will and left it all to Willy then she wasn't in her right mind, anybody would tell you that!" Her sobs quite overcame her, and Lily and Dolly, after giving her a frightened look, flung themselves at her and began wailing too.

Uncomfortably, the Overses eyed them and

then each other. "She didn't leave it to me . . ." Willy was beginning.

"There's the shop bell," said Mr. Overs hastily, and hurried out.

"I can hear Uncle Harold's voice," announced George, who of all the assembly in the parlor had remained the most detached. He jumped from his chair and went to peer through the lace curtain into the shop. "Yes, it's him and Stan all right, and he looks like he's in a state!"

Uncle Harold, when he pushed through into the parlor an instant later, did indeed look like he was in a state. His face was mottled red and purple and he was puffing and snorting like a blown cab horse. But Auntie Kitty saw none of this, she was still weeping loudly into her handkerchief with Lily and Dolly sniveling, one on each shoulder.

"What's going on here?" he demanded.

Auntie Kitty lifted her head and stared at him vacantly. "Oh, Harold, after all these years, and us going over so regular, too, and after all she said, Auntie took leave of her senses at the last and left it all to Willy!" She gave a shuddering sigh and the tears began again.

"I tell you, I wouldn't have it if she had," shouted Willy. "And I told her so, didn't I, Father?" he appealed to Mr. Overs who was stand-

ing at the parlor door just behind Uncle Harold.

"That's right," Mr. Overs began, "Willy stood up to her a fair treat; it made me proud to see him. 'I'm not having it', he said . . ."

He was allowed to go no further. "Oh, stop it, all of you," exploded Uncle Harold. "It don't matter who she left it to and who she didn't, the dogs have ate it all!" He sat down heavily in the chair that George had left.

There was a stupefied silence in the parlor. The female Sowters, startled out of their sobs, stared at him with sagging chins.

"The dogs?" said Mr. Overs weakly.

"The dogs she kept to guard her money have ate her money. That's what I'm telling you."

"But isn't there any left for us, Pa?" said Dolly shrilly.

"It wasn't *your* money, you weren't going to have none," Stan told her roughly.

"We was going to have black merino dresses with braid on, Lil and me, made by Kendal's," insisted Dolly. "Weren't we, Ma?"

"And I'm telling you that there won't be merino nor braid nor nothing of that sort for anybody," shouted her father. "The dogs have ate it all, do you hear? There isn't anything to pay for the funeral even, as far as I can see."

"Was it those dogs Willy and me heard on Thursday, tearing and scratching at the back?" Mr. Overs asked. "My word they were savage 'uns. I wouldn't like to have them in my house."

"That's them. The old woman that looks after the place says she was told to leave the door open last night so's Auntie could hear 'em at it. Then Auntie said she wanted to see them for herself, so up they came and ate up all the money that Auntie had on her bed."

"Yes, she had it all in banknotes." Mr. Overs wagged his head sagely. "I could have told her."

"And the shock of it killed her. That's what Hannah Raffetty said when Stan and me got there just now. She sent a boy to fetch us early this morning, but he couldn't say nothing about how she passed away."

"Well, now," said Mr. Overs, "it's a judgment if ever there was one, not to set our hopes on earthly things."

And to this the Sowters had nothing to say. Events, it seemed, had overpowered all five of them.

The Overs and the Sowters did not meet for talking purposes until after the funeral the following week. There was no family gathering of the usual kind; Uncle Harold had said he wasn't going to pay for sherry and biscuits all around out of his own pocket, and there certainly wasn't any money left by the deceased to pay for it. So they walked back from Rusholme Cemetery, four adults, five children all in black, in a straggling, silent procession.

"Why don't you come in and have a cup of tea?" said Mrs. Overs when they neared the turn for Audley Street. "You'll need something after that."

She had, however, prepared something far more elaborate than a cup of tea, and the parlor table had been laid with the best china and a substantial showing of scones and jams and preserves and breads and a fine seed cake and parkin.

"And how did Willy get on at the Northern Star?" asked Auntie Kitty at the end of the meal where everybody had eaten a lot but said very little. "Didn't you say you was going to take him to the Northern Star to fix him up with a job for when he leaves school?" She said it in the tone of one who does not really want to know but is forced into asking for politeness' sake. "Why, I do believe you were going to take him along that very Saturday that poor Auntie passed away."

"Oh, the Northern Star!" said Mr. Overs airily. "Yes, the Northern Star. Well, I wrote a little note to Mr. Ramsbottom thanking him for his trouble and all that, and saying that we had other plans for Willy. Willy's going to go to Manchester Grammar School, and then if he goes on doing well, to a university. I've been talking it over with his schoolmaster who tells me Willy's promising, very promising indeed. He has the makings of a fine scholar, has Willy. He reads all the time. You should see the sort of books he reads! And the way he handled that lord out Stockport way, and the letter he wrote! My word, I was proud of him. He only needs a bit more learning, I said to myself, and he'll be able to hold any lord you like in the palm of his hand."

Willy was thrown quite off his balance by this astonishing piece of information and could only stare at his father, bewildered. Mr. Overs had a knack of springing surprises on his family, but this beat them all. Of course they had missed that appointment at the Northern Star on Saturday, but Willy had put it down to the upset of Miss Chaffey's death. And here was his father announcing a complete reversal of all his previous plans, and behaving breezily as though it had been his settled policy for a lifetime. But wholly unprepared though they might be, the Overs family responded magnificently to the lead he had given.

They would at all costs present a united front to the Sowters.

"Didn't Mr. Church say as how Willy could get a scholarship?" said George.

"Mr. Church has always thought well of Willy. But then of course, so did Auntie, though she only saw him at the end." Mrs. Overs wiped her eyes. "She said he was a proper Chaffey, Alfred says; said she'd know him anywhere."

"Did you see Uncle Harold's face?" George said gleefully when the Sowters had taken their leave a little later. "Sour as six lemons, it was. Father, is Willy really going to a *university*!—why, not even Mr. Goodsire at the chapel's been to one of *them*!"

"I see no reason why he shouldn't get scholarships there too." Mr. Overs stuck his thumbs in the pockets of his waistcoat. "Willy's a thruster, a real go-getter. I can see that by the way he's struck out for himself, and the way he put that lord in his place. I'll remember that to my dying day."

"But what about the niche in the town hall, Father?" persisted George. "Didn't you want Will to go to the Northern Star so's he could get in one of them?"

"There are other ways of getting that," said Mr. Overs loftily. "Besides, you never know, Willy might go beyond it. He might . . ." he hesitated and took a deep breath, "he might even get a statue—in London."

"Cor—our Will?" said George unbelievingly. "Tell you what though, it were good on Sunday, weren't it, having a first Sunday tea, and none of the Trafford lot there for once. Wish it could happen every time."

"Don't you worry about the Trafford lot," his father told him. "The Overs are on top now. Willy's going to see to that."